Other books by Charles Haddad

Meet Calliope Day

Captain Tweakerbeak's Revenge

Calliope
Falls ...
in Love?

by Charles Haddad
illustrated by Margeaux Lucas

DELACORTE PRESS

Published by
Delacorte Press
an imprint of
Random House Children's Books
a division of Random House, Inc.
New York

Visit us on the Web! www.randomhouse.com/kids
Educators and librarians, for a variety of teaching tools, visit us at www.randomhouse.com/teachers

Library of Congress Cataloging-in-Publication Data
Haddad, Charles (Charles Harold)
Calliope day falls . . . in love? / Charles Haddad.
p. cm.
Summary: While trying to discover who left a love poem in Noreen's ice cream during a blackout at the roller rink, fourth-grader Calliope Day learns some very interesting facts about boys.
ISBN 0-385-73070-5 (trade) — ISBN 0-385-90100-3 (GLB)
[1. Interpersonal relations—Fiction. 2. Poetry—Fiction. 3. Loveletters—Fiction. 4. Letters—Fiction. 5. Humorous stories.] I. Title.
PZ7 .H1163 Cal 2003
[Fic]—dc21

2002013058

The text of this book is set in 12-point Figural.
Book design by Melissa J Knight

Printed in the United States of America
May 2003
10 9 8 7 6 5 4 3 2 1
BVG

Calliope Day
Falls . . .
in Love?

No Gentleman

Calliope Day wasn't fooled by Rodney's greasy tweed jacket and lopsided bow tie. She knew he was no gentleman. That's why she eyed him as he kept glancing over his shoulder at her.

It was a wintry Sunday afternoon in late March and Spackle's indoor roller rink throbbed with shouting, skating, shoving kids. Calliope glided hand in hand with her best friend, Noreen Catherwood.

Ahead of Calliope and Noreen skated Rodney. Again he glanced back at his fourth-grade classmates.

What is he up to? Calliope wondered as she wobbled along in white skates scuffed nearly black from a winter of hard use.

Noreen's black skates, on the other hand, still shone as if brand-new. Calliope suspected that Noreen let her maid, Louisa, polish them every Saturday night. It looked like Louisa had also ironed Noreen's white blouse, which stood erect, as if at attention. And, while she was at it, maybe Louisa had ironed Noreen's ponytail as well. Not a hair strayed from the black ribbon that pulled back Noreen's brown hair. In its rigid perfection, the ponytail was a tempting target. What boy wouldn't want to give it a good yank? Was that what Rodney had in mind?

Rodney had given up any pretense of stealth and now stared directly at Calliope and Noreen. Calliope squeezed her friend's hand to reassure her. But, truth be told, Calliope needed reassuring as much as Noreen needed Calliope. After a winter of Sundays at the skating rink, Calliope had learned she was better at falling down than circling around and around. There wasn't a tree in South Orange or Maplewood she couldn't monkey up in her bright red Keds. Yet in skates she careened into the rink's low wall and toppled over when trying to stop. Yes, it was better to skate clutching Noreen's hand.

That seemed especially true now, given that Rodney was chuckling to himself as if enjoying a private joke, probably at Calliope's expense. He had been tormenting her since kindergarten.

Calliope couldn't understand why Rodney hated her so much. They had so much in common! They both lived in the same neighborhood of simple houses in the shadowed valley of South Mountain. *And*, as the youngest in their families, they were both tormented by older brothers.

Rodney peeled away from the line of skaters circling the rink, and looped into the empty space in the middle.

Calliope wondered if Noreen noticed Rodney's troubling shift in behavior. She glanced at her friend. Sharp nose raised ever so slightly, Noreen gazed ahead and smiled faintly as if bemused by the picture of herself mingling with kids whose parents had to drive their own cars.

Noreen, of course, traveled to and from the roller rink and Indian Trail Elementary School in a red chauffeured Mercedes the size of a small school bus. Did Rodney know this? Calliope doubted it, given the blackened windows of the Mercedes. You could see just fine out of those windows, but no one could see in. Calliope knew. Not only had she ridden in the Mercedes, but she had been to Noreen's castle of a house perched high atop South Mountain.

Out of all the kids at school, rich and poor, brainy and boneheaded, Noreen had anointed Calliope as her best—and as far as Calliope could tell, only—friend. It was a friendship that left kids and teachers chewing the eraser ends of their No. 2 pencils in befuddlement. Even Calliope didn't quite get it.

Here We Go Again

Rodney was eyeing them with a devilish smile. He'd now looped around to face Calliope and Noreen and then dropped to a crouch. The better, apparently, to gather the speed to knock them over like a couple of bowling pins.

Calliope couldn't skate well enough, especially with Noreen in hand, to weave out of the circling line and make a clean escape.

That left only one defense: shrieking. And any girl who heard another one shrieking felt obliged to join in. So if Calliope could shriek loud enough to attract the attention of the other girls in the rink, she just might repel the oncoming Rodney.

Calliope gulped a chestful of air, threw back her head and let loose. Her throat vibrated like the strings of a guitar. Calliope imagined that her shriek was rattling the crystal ball dangling over the rink.

But that was just in Calliope's imagination. In fact, the din of creaking wheels and giggling kids swallowed up her call for help. No girls rallied to her defense, save one. Noreen turned, forehead wrinkled with irritation, to glare at Calliope. Then she saw Rodney and began to shriek, too.

Their shrieking made Calliope's ears ring but it didn't seem to faze Rodney. On he raced, head down and grinning.

Calliope couldn't bear to watch another moment. She threw up her hands, never letting go of Noreen. A veil of fingers hid Rodney from view but Calliope could still smell him. Her nostrils twitched from a whiff of his sweaty tweed. And then his elbow clipped her on the hip. Calliope spun around, spinning Noreen with her. Thankfully neither of them fell—this time.

"Watch it, Rodney!" Calliope yelled. She watched as Rodney gracefully skated away without bumping a single skater. On the other side of the rink Rodney stopped, grinning.

If Rodney had meant to impress Calliope or Noreen, he'd failed. Noreen narrowed her eyes in a withering look that could have silenced a laughing hyena.

But Noreen's disapproval did not deter Rodney. In fact, it seemed to egg him on. Again and again he whizzed through the other skaters to hit Calliope just enough to spin her. It was as if he was trying to knock Calliope free of Noreen. But Calliope held Noreen's hand even tighter, as the two of them spun around and around. Noreen's face had turned a sickly green and Calliope was so dizzy now that one more bump would surely topple her.

Calliope seriously considered just throwing herself down on the rink floor and getting it over with. What stopped her from such a humiliating surrender was a most unusual sight. Careening in front of her was Kevin Jefferson, boy brainiac of the fourth grade. Calliope had never seen him at the rink before. And it didn't look like Kevin had skated much. In fact it looked like he had never skated at all. His arms windmilled as if trying to reverse direction, and his mouth was shaped in the O of a silent cry.

Kevin might have been the worst skater Calliope had ever seen, but she was still glad to see him. That was because Kevin veered into Rodney's path.

Rodney and Kevin went down in a tangle of arms and skates.

Calliope and Noreen didn't linger to savor Rodney's takedown. Hand in hand, the two of them stumbled out of the line of skaters. Walking, however awkward, seemed safer than trying to skate away. In the rink's adjoining cafeteria, the girls stopped and hugged. "Boys!" wheezed Noreen.

Calliope couldn't agree more. She'd come to regard boys as you would stray dogs. Some boys looked friendly enough from afar but you'd learned that, not only might they bite, you never knew when that bite would come. And you rarely knew why they bit.

Calliope eyed the bustling cafeteria, crowded with rolling boys with wandering eyes and idle hands. Who among them would lunge for Noreen's ponytail next?

Not the Proudest Moment

As moments go it wasn't Calliope's proudest. She was still shuddering at the memory of herself shrieking, eyes covered, at Rodney's approach.

To console herself Calliope had ordered a heaping bowl of her favorite ice cream, tutti-frutti surprise, vanilla ice cream dyed red, white and blue. It was pricey but Calliope bought two scoops. Its brilliant multicolored swirl made other kids stop and gawk at your bowl—and that alone was worth the money to Calliope.

She and Noreen had secured a low table at the back of the rink's cafeteria. From there they had a sweeping view of the swirl of kids on the rink in front of them. No boy could swoop in without the girls seeing him first.

Calliope doubted anyone could see them now, anyway. The lights had been dimmed for the big dance number. Overhead the crystal ball flashed, turning the bodies of skaters into flickering silhouettes moving in time to the thumping beat of the loud music. Calliope swayed her head to the beat.

"You'd better eat your ice cream," chided Noreen.

Calliope squinted at her bowl of tutti-frutti. Her scoops had melted into a rusty-colored soup. She must have been silently stewing over her brush with Rodney for some time. "Look who's talking," said Calliope, pointing at Noreen's melting green ice cream.

Noreen didn't answer. She sat upright, with pinky raised, hovering over her bowl. Every now and then she plucked out a green sliver and laid it on a napkin alongside her bowl, where nuts lay in neat rows.

Noreen could have saved herself the trouble of denutting her pistachio ice cream by ordering strawberry or chocolate. But no, that would have been too easy. Noreen wanted the taste of pistachio minus the lumpy imperfection of the nuts. That was Noreen, thought Calliope with a sigh. Always trying to remake the world to her liking.

For a moment Calliope considered lifting Noreen by the frilly white collar of her blouse, guiding her back to the counter and making her trade in the melting bowl of pistachio for French vanilla. Now, that was the flavor for Noreen. Rich and creamy, it tasted like a million bucks.

Calliope slurped a spoonful of soupy tutti-frutti. The creamy ice cream was working to salve her wounded pride. At least Rodney had given her a new adventure to regale kids with at lunch on Monday. Of course she would have to fiddle with the facts some. There was no way Calliope wanted anyone to think a boy had rescued her, especially a runt like Kevin. In her new and improved version, Calliope would stick out her skated foot, tripping Rodney. He'd go sailing.

Only one thing troubled her. What would make the best clincher, sending Rodney into the rink's low wall or over it?

Calliope's dad would have known how to end her tall tale. Dad's stubbly face, with his yellowing teeth and oniony breath, shimmered in the back of her imagination. What a storyteller he had been! Again she heard him tell the story of Iggy McNewton, the boy who could shrink himself down inside an atom. There Iggy befriended all the protons, neutrons and electrons. It was an unforgettable story and Calliope had amazed her first-grade teacher with her mastery of basic physics. Dad was always doing stuff like that, spooning her wise tidbits with his big yarns and practical jokes.

Now Dad was gone. He'd died three years ago of cancer. But his love of storytelling lived on in Calliope. How could it not, seeing as he'd named her after the Greek muse of epic poetry? Muses, Dad had explained, were these nine sister spirits who worked for the big boss of all Greek gods, Zeus. He commanded them to inspire the humans to greatness. If by greatness Zeus meant getting people to stand up and take notice of you, Calliope was doing her best.

Calliope couldn't wait to tell her story of besting Rodney at the rink. She was sure everyone would laugh. Everyone except Noreen, that is. Calliope could see her now, looking down that sharp nose, insisting that that was not the way it happened at all. "Hey," Calliope would counter, "it's my story. I can remember it any way I want to."

This would surely set them squabbling and the thought of it made Calliope smile. Fighting with Noreen was such fun. It was like squaring off in a game of foursquare with your toughest opponent. Except Noreen preferred words to rubber balls.

You couldn't find two more different opponents than Calliope and Noreen. They were like rubber band and ruler, Calliope thought with a smile. Noreen was always measuring to see how far Calliope had crossed the line of what Noreen deemed proper behavior for a young lady. And Calliope was forever stretching to see how far she could reach beyond the last notch on Noreen's ruler.

It didn't sound like they'd get along at all. But, in fact, Noreen loved it when Calliope made up whoppers, snuck pink plastic fangs into class or waggled Barbie heads on the tip of her pinky. Why, Calliope wasn't sure. The best she could figure was this: It was no fun being a ruler without something to measure. And, thanks to Noreen, Calliope had learned it was a lot more fun stretching the rules if someone protested.

Truth was, Noreen paid a lot more attention to Calliope than her own family. It wasn't that her mother and two teenage brothers didn't love Calliope. They just didn't have the time to show it. Mom worked. Calliope's brother Jonah was busy going to Seton Hall University and her brother Frederick—well, who knows what he did. He surely didn't spend a lot of time at home, except for eating and sleeping. Which meant that Calliope got stuck with most of the housecleaning and laundry.

Harrumph. This was not what she wanted to be thinking about on a Sunday afternoon. What she wanted to do was make Noreen laugh.

Noreen Honks

You'd never guess from her twig of a body that Noreen could honk like a goose. But when Calliope made her laugh, she could. Making Noreen laugh wasn't easy. Luckily, Calliope was good at it.

She scanned the rink now for inspiration. There weren't any piles of toppled skaters, but she did see something that caught her eye. It was Kevin, who sat alone atop a carpeted bench. Strewn across the bench were the parts of his disassembled skate. He'd apparently figured out not only how to unscrew the blade but also how to detach the sole of the skate and its eyelets. Twisting a curl of his hair, Kevin squatted hunched over his knees, studying the parts laid out before him. The poor skate reminded Calliope of the scarecrow in *The Wizard of Oz* after the flying monkey demons have knocked the stuffing out of him.

Calliope chuckled and stabbed a finger toward the hunched figure on the carpeted bench. "Oh, look, Boy Brainiac is reassembling his skate into a death laser."

"Get out," scoffed Noreen. But she did look up from her ice cream. Her eyes narrowed sharply, cutting through the rink's gloom. At the sight of Kevin, Noreen smiled, if only slightly.

Well, that's a start, thought Calliope. But now she needed a little more help. She got it when a boy skater collided with Kevin's bench and toppled face first into his disassembled skate.

Calliope glanced at Noreen. Her left cheek dimpled but she didn't start honking.

Kevin wasn't helping much. Why didn't he yelp in protest or roll off the bench in a tangle of arms and legs with the colliding skater? Instead he ignored the boy crumpled at his feet and his eyes remained glued to the skate. Who did he think he was, a real-life Dexter, boy scientist?

Calliope moved on. Aha! Now, here was something sure to make Noreen at least smirk, if not honk with laughter.

Rodney was perched on the corner of a table full of girls, yakking away while trying to straighten his bow tie, which kept flopping to one side and then the other. All the while he kept an eye on a heaping bowl of ice cream in front of a girl named Carol Anne. She was the one girl in school who was richer than Noreen. At least that was what Carol Anne said. Noreen despised her the way you did a fly that wouldn't buzz off.

"What are they talking about?" wondered Calliope aloud.

"Who?" asked Noreen, looking up.

Calliope pointed toward Carol Anne.

"Oh, that's easy to guess," said Noreen. "Rodney's trying to sweet-talk Carol Anne out of her ice cream."

"She'll never buy it."

"Oh no?" Noreen nodded toward Carol Anne as she spooned ice cream into Rodney's mouth.

"Oooh," Calliope and Noreen groaned in unison.

"I thought Carol Anne had more sense," said Calliope.

Noreen smiled. "She reminds me of Ashley."

Ashley was Noreen's older sister. Calliope had never met her. She'd left for college before Calliope and Noreen had become friends. "What do you mean?"

"Boys were always trying to get Ashley to look at them."

"How?"

"They'd throw paper airplanes at her, bump into her, send her notes. Ashley liked it."

Calliope nodded. She'd seen the kids at the back of the school cafeteria who were always trading scraps of notebook paper. In fact, she'd once intercepted one of those scraps. Scrawled in boy handwriting was "I see London, I see France. I see Sheryl's underpants." Calliope grimaced at the memory.

"Even if boys made fun of her underpants?"

"Didn't seem to faze her."

"Well, no boy is ever going to make fun of my underpants—and live!"

Noreen shrugged.

"What, you'd let them?"

"No . . ."

"No, but . . ."

"Love does funny things to a girl," Noreen said with a sigh.

"Not this girl," said Calliope, glaring at Rodney as he prepared to accept another spoonful of ice cream with a big smile.

Thank goodness at that moment a skater bumped straight into Carol Anne, who lurched forward, smooshing her ice cream into Rodney's eye.

Calliope heard a strange if familiar sound. It came from her right, where Noreen was doubled over, her nostrils flared in honking laughter.

The Red Note

Noreen suddenly stopped honking. She shot up out of her seat, legs crossed. Clearly she had to use the restroom—and pronto.

Poor Noreen, thought Calliope. She couldn't so much as giggle without suddenly having to pee. Calliope suspected that Noreen's mother, Mrs. Catherwood, had somehow wired Noreen's bladder to her funny bone. Mrs. Catherwood didn't approve of her daughter having too much fun. That wasn't very ladylike. Well, Noreen didn't look very ladylike right now, hobbling with her legs crossed toward the bathroom at the back of the rink.

As Noreen entered the girls' room there was a loud *pzzt.* Then the rink went dark. Calliope heard the thuds of skaters slamming into one another and the wall. Girls shrieked, although more in fun than in fright. Spackle's roller rink lost its lights at least once every Sunday. Calliope wondered if the teenagers manning the rink didn't blow the fuse on purpose just to juice up the day.

Any minute now, Calliope said to herself as she sat alone in the dark waiting for the lights to flicker back on. She began to fidget. Not in fear, of course, but in boredom. What she needed was a distraction.

Calliope's eyes, now used to the dark, wandered to the bowl of soupy green ice cream beside her. She'd always wondered if Noreen's favorite flavor of ice cream really tasted like pistachios. Why not give it a try? Noreen wouldn't return until the lights came back on.

Calliope spooned up a mouthful of the pistachio ice cream. Not bad. Not bad at all. She began shoveling it in.

Suddenly there was another loud *pzzt* and the lights flickered and then came back on.

Uh-oh, thought Calliope. Caught red-handed! She was hunched over Noreen's bowl, soupy green ice cream dribbling down her chin. Calliope dropped her spoon into the bowl and looked around quickly.

There was no sign of Noreen, thank goodness. But what was this? A red paper square no bigger than a bite-sized Nestlé's Crunch bar was balanced on the lip of Noreen's bowl.

At first Calliope figured the paper must have been a wayward missile thrown by one boy at another. Or *she* could have been the target. A lone girl such as herself was a tempting mark for a table of boys. Calliope scowled at the tables around her, but she didn't see any snickering boys.

Now that she thought about it, the paper couldn't have been thrown. It wasn't crumpled into a ball or folded into the shape of an airplane. And, if thrown, the paper surely would have landed in Noreen's bowl, splattering Calliope with ice cream.

whatever

But then, if not a missile, what was it? Calliope glanced around quickly. There was still no sign of Noreen. Calliope picked up the red square of paper. Her fingers felt lines of indentations. Could it be a note? Her fingers, fumbling in haste, struggled to unfold the paper.

Inside she found twelve lines. The first was perfectly centered, but each following line drifted a little farther to the right. The type looked like it was sliding off the page.

And another odd thing. The lines looked stamped, not printed out as from a computer. How strange, thought Calliope at first, but then she figured it out. The author had used a typewriter. Her college brother, Jonah, had one in his room at home. You didn't even have to plug it in. As a small girl she had loved to sit in bed with the small typewriter in her lap, banging on the keys. It stamped out letters just like the ones in this note.

By now Calliope had forgotten all about Noreen. Her eyes began to devour the first lines on the paper.

```
Your knees are knobby,
 and your skating I fear
  a bit wobbly . . .
```

Calliope cupped a hand to her mouth, stifling a laugh, and read on.

```
You fell once or twice
  mumbled something un-nice . . .
```

Wasn't that just like Noreen? She had a way of putting you in your place without ever uttering a nasty word. Calliope read on.

Let them laugh, let them stare,
now why would you care?
When you're Noreen, my Noreen,
you skate as you please.
Noreen, my Noreen,
would you please skate with me?

Calliope's face flushed the color of the note in her hand. This was not some throwaway insult. It was a real love poem! Like the ones her dad used to make up about her. Again she saw Dad's round face bristling with gray stubble. Mouth cocked back in a half grin, he teased Calliope with his latest rhyme about her. She was his exotic butterfly Leopia Calloria, his playground Tarzan, his poet monkey. Her heart skipped like a flat stone across still water as she realized that some faceless boy among the mob of Sunday skaters had noticed Noreen and Calliope wobbling side by side. And he'd chosen to fall in love with Noreen. Calliope felt the passing rush of Cupid's arrow brush her cheek.

You should be grateful, Calliope told herself. Who wanted some boy tagging around after her? Yet Calliope felt anything but grateful. Instead she found herself comparing her knees to those of Noreen's. Weren't Calliope's just as knobby? And surely she fell as often as Noreen. *More* on a bad day!

Calliope's grip tightened on the note until it began to crumple. She considered shredding it and scattering the note's words to the swirl of the rink. But she couldn't bring herself to destroy it. She kept reading the verse over and over.

"What's that?"

The voice came from behind Calliope and she immediately recognized it as Noreen's.

"Ah . . . ah . . . ," Calliope stammered as she stuffed the red note into her pocket. Recovering her composure, she seized the offensive and questioned Noreen back. "Where have you been?"

"Huh?" said Noreen, caught off guard. Then she brightened. "You won't believe what happened to me."

"Tell me, tell me," said Calliope, propping her elbows up on the table. She rested her head in her upturned hands, gazing up at Noreen, all ears.

Calliope-rella

The rink's blackout had stranded Noreen with a bunch of other girls in the bathroom. When the lights flickered back on they'd found a girl passed out on the floor. The other girls had screamed at the sight of the little body sprawled at their feet, but not Noreen. She had taken control.

Noreen dispatched a girl to fetch water, which Noreen splashed in the fainted girl's face. The poor thing woke up sobbing and Noreen directed another two girls to hug and comfort her. In no time at all the fainted girl was ready to walk out of the bathroom by herself. Noreen had saved her the embarrassment of having to be carried out in front of the whole rink.

All in all, pretty impressive, thought Calliope. You could tell Noreen thought so, too. She was so wrapped up in telling her story that she'd forgotten about the red note.

Not so Calliope. A sharp corner of the note dug into her thigh, as if urging her to surrender it to its rightful owner. But she couldn't bring herself to do it.

Was she jealous? Well, maybe a tad. Her real concern was this: What if Noreen went gaga over the note, hunted down its author and forgot all about Calliope? It sounded far-fetched, but Calliope wasn't taking any chances.

At least that was what Calliope told herself as she walked home, skates strung across her neck. It was late afternoon. She hopped from slab to slab of the sidewalk and glanced up at the tall trees that lined her route. Their leafless limbs looked like long-nailed fingers clawing at the gloomy sky.

Calliope shuddered and began to regret having turned down a ride home in Noreen's chauffeured car. Yet how could she have accepted? It would have been just like Noreen to remember halfway home her glimpse of the red note in Calliope's hand. Then Calliope would have had to give it back.

Ahead Calliope saw the Musclemobile. That was what her mother called her brother Frederick's 1967 orange Camaro. He only used it to take girls out on dates. But without fail the Camaro would break down and Frederick and his date would have to push it home.

Maybe that was why Frederick was always dating a new girl. Of every new girl who walked in the door Calliope would innocently ask, "Where's What's-her-name?" The question never failed to make both Frederick and the girl scowl—the girl at Frederick and Frederick at Calliope. Frederick might scowl and clench his fist but he never retaliated. Not with the girl, and often Mom, standing there. But he would strike back later, by spiking Calliope's orange juice with a dollop of ketchup or hiding a rotten banana in her room.

Calliope walked past the Camaro and turned down the warped concrete walkway that led to her purple house with turquoise shutters. As she clattered onto the small porch the front door opened, revealing a woman holding a carpet sweeper. It wasn't a maid, like at Noreen's house, it was just Calliope's mom.

Mom peered over Calliope's shoulder and into the street as if expecting to find something.

Calliope knew her mom was looking for Noreen's car. "I decided to walk home," explained Calliope.

Mom studied Calliope a moment longer and then handed her daughter the carpet sweeper as if passing the baton in a relay race.

Calliope accepted it dutifully. She felt proud that Mom had come to count on her to help clean the house. But then again, who else was there? Neither of her brothers had so much as looked at a carpet sweeper since age sixteen. And they were too big now to boss around.

"I finished the downstairs," said Mom as she threw on a long cloth coat. She usually left to go grocery shopping when Calliope returned home on Sundays.

Calliope nodded, heading toward the stairs.

"And, of course, there's the laundry," said Mom as she went out the front door.

Oh, joy.

Poetry by Flashlight

"Your knees are knobby," Calliope recited to herself, fingering the red note that was now in the pocket of her pajamas. "And your skating, I fear, a bit wobbly." She tittered in the dark, lying faceup in her bed. Who in the world could have written such words? No boy she knew came to mind.

As far as she knew, boys didn't write. They drew jet fighters and snarling space monsters. And their pictures never included girls—unless as evil princesses who ended up blasted to bits.

Not all boys wanted to blast girls. Her brother Frederick, for one, enjoyed taking them out on dates in his Camaro.

For her brother Jonah, girls were curiosities, like a cat clock with rolling eyes. They were fun to wonder about but he never took them seriously.

Neither her brothers nor the boys at school who only saw girls as evil princesses seemed like the type to write love poetry. Calliope sighed. It was such a mystery.

It wasn't every day she was stumped. She considered herself a regular Nate the Great. Why, just last week, she had correctly fingered Thomas as the culprit who'd pasted Noreen's spelling homework upside down under her desk.

But fingering the mystery poet of this note would require a detective mind greater than her own. Luckily she knew just where to find it. First, though, she'd have to wait for her family to fall asleep.

Struggling to stay awake, Calliope listened as her family nodded off one by one. The first to go was Mom. She popped in to kiss Calliope good-night en route to her own bedroom next door. Next Calliope heard Jonah flop on the living room couch beneath her. Jonah always said he was going to study but Calliope knew better. After a while she heard his heavy book clunk to the floor, signaling he had fallen asleep. Now, what would Frederick do?

He answered by clumping down the attic stairs. Minutes later Calliope heard the Camaro on the street outside her bedroom window rattle to life. Ah, Frederick must have a date. Which means he'd be out for the evening. Ever since he'd received his driver's license, Frederick had turned into a bat on the weekends, sleeping during the day and staying out much of the night. Calliope knew, because she was a bit of a night prowler herself.

As the rattle of the Camaro faded into the night, Calliope slipped out of bed. She scampered down the stairs, halting at the bottom to peer into the living room. There Jonah indeed slumbered on the couch.

Calliope breezed past him, ruffling his dirty

brown hair, then flew through the kitchen and into a small dinette, where a cage sat atop several crates pushed against some back windows. Unlatching the cage, Calliope reached inside and retrieved a large fluffy white bunny with one black eye. She stuffed him under one arm and then scurried back upstairs into her bed.

"What do you think, Mortimer?" asked Calliope, pushing the red note under the bunny's twitching nose. She lay cheek to cheek with Mortimer, scrunched at the bottom of her bed under the covers. One hand flattened the note on the sheets while the other trained a flashlight on the poem.

Mortimer pressed his wet nose against the note.

"Here's my theory," said Calliope. "I don't think the author is a boy at all. I think it's Carol Anne."

Not only did Carol Anne think she was richer than Noreen, she thought she was more proper, too. She and Noreen were always trying to outlady each other, vying, for example, to see who could shine her shoes brighter. It would be just like Carol Anne to make fun of Noreen's skating.

"Well?" said Calliope, looking triumphantly at Mortimer.

Mortimer sat impassively, obviously unimpressed by Calliope's theory. You know what? Mortimer was right, Calliope decided. Carol Anne had no sense of humor. And her rhyming? Calliope winced, remembering Carol Anne reading one of her poems in class. Besides, if Carol Anne were teasing Noreen, she

wouldn't have stopped at the knees. No girl would have. She would have poked fun at Noreen from head to toe.

But if not Carol Anne, who? Who?

Calliope rolled over onto her back and closed her eyes. She pulled Mortimer onto her chest and tried to picture a boy who'd write poetry. An image flickered across the back of her eyelids but it wasn't of any boy.

Again she saw the bristling round face of her father. Calliope's dad was as alive as ever in her imagination. More so in some ways. Dad had become an outlined figure in a coloring book where her imagination could paint him in any way she chose. She wondered now, for instance, who Dad had been as a boy. Had he written poems to girls? She bet he had.

Calliope pictured him now as a fourth grader at the roller rink. He sat at a center table, flocked by girls. Each begged him to write a poem about her, but Dad politely declined. He'd only write for the special girl with the frizzy blond hair and red Keds.

Calliope felt her face flush in the darkness under the covers. Had her father come back to life in the body of some little boy? But why, then, was he writing to Noreen and not to her?

The Beauty Costume

The morning light splashed into Calliope's face like a bucket of cold water.

"There you are!" Calliope heard her mother exclaim.

"Geez, Mom," croaked Calliope. She wrinkled her eyes shut against the light, and her hands groped for blankets that no longer covered her.

"And I thought you'd escaped and run away," continued Mom.

"Huh?" Calliope turned to squint up at her mother, who stood above her, holding back the blankets and pointing at Mortimer, still nestled on Calliope's chest.

Calliope bolted upright, hugging Mortimer. "Don't be mad," she sputtered, knowing full well Mortimer wasn't allowed in her room after bedtime. "I couldn't have fallen asleep without him. He was my blankie." By blankie, Calliope meant the threadbare baby blanket she'd slept with until a year ago, when it had unraveled in her fingers and her mom had made her throw the pieces away.

Mom eyed Mortimer and sighed. "What's that in your blankie's mouth?"

Calliope glanced down to see the red note protruding from Mortimer's whiskers. He'd already gnawed off a corner and his wriggling nose inched toward the poem. "Oh, that," said Calliope, yanking the note out of Mortimer's mouth. She heard it tear but didn't look, instead crumpling the note and tossing it behind her. "It's nothing."

"Nothing?"

Calliope ignored the question.

Mom glanced down at her watch and frowned. She had already lost interest in the note. Without looking up, she turned toward the door. As she exited Calliope's room, she called out, "You'd better put your blankie back in his cage or you're going to be late for school."

Calliope set Mortimer down on the bed and rolled onto the floor. Lying on her belly, she reached under her bed and retrieved the note. "Oh, Mortimer," she groaned as she sat up. The note was torn nearly in half.

Lovingly Calliope carried the note over to a card table opposite her bed. Strewn across the top were paper, crayons, pencils and—bingo—tape. She taped the note back together the best she could. The words didn't quite match up, but no matter. She now knew the poem by heart.

Calliope closed her eyes and tried again to conjure up the mystery poet but the only face that drifted across the back of her eyelids was a boyish-looking Dad. Could there really be a boy out there like him? The thought gave Calliope goose bumps. This was a boy she had to find.

Calliope slumped in the metal chair. On the card table in front of her was a flyer for the French Canadian circus troupe Cirque du Soleil. It featured a girl acrobat in a red-and-white-checkered leotard and tutu. Her blond hair was a forest of little upright ponytails tied off in red ribbons. She gazed ahead, sphinxlike in whiteface and big ruby red lips.

That stony unreadable face gave Calliope a wonderful idea. She trembled with excitement. There was no need to hunt down the mystery poet. She'd draw him to her. Like this acrobat! Calliope would make herself up to look so interesting that the mystery poet would forget all about Noreen. Ha! Knobby knees were nothing compared to what Calliope would offer him to write about.

Brothers!

Only something truly special could distract Frederick from a sizzling pan of steak and eggs. That was how Calliope knew her outfit was a stroke of genius. Frederick looked up from his frying pan as she paraded into the kitchen with Mortimer under an arm. He stood silent at the stove in his standard uniform of black boots, untucked T-shirt and army jacket. A spatula dangled from his hand. An egg popped.

"What?" said Calliope, stopping. Slowly she turned, modeling her outfit for Frederick. She wore baggy red pants festooned with colored balloons, and a pink sweatshirt that said "Whatever" in black ink. On one foot was a blue sock in a red Ked, while the other sported a red sock in a blue Ked.

But the clothes weren't the best part of her outfit. That dangled like a tail from a rear belt loop on her pants. It was a charm Calliope had whipped up in a flash of inspiration. She'd woven the hair of three Barbie heads—a blonde, a brunette and a redhead—into a heart-shaped knot. Threaded through the knot were little silver bells.

Calliope shook her bottom and the bells tinkled.

Resist that, Mr. Mystery Poet. This charm was Calliope's poet bait and she planned to tinkle her way across the neighborhood on the way to school.

Already the three-headed charm was working its magic. At the sound of the bells Jonah emerged in the doorway of the pantry behind Calliope. He held a brimming jar of homemade granola and stuffed handfuls of it into his mouth.

Calliope shook her head as she watched Jonah rain bits of oatmeal and nuts onto the floor around his feet. Of course she would be the one who'd have to clean up his mess later. Brothers!

Jonah studied Calliope for a long, munching moment. Then he lowered his hand and spoke. "Running away to the circus, are we?"

Was that a compliment or a put-down? It was hard to tell with Jonah. His words sounded sweet, yet they often made Calliope wince, like he was offering her a crowbar dipped in chocolate.

"Maybe, what's it to you?" said Calliope, trying to tease a compliment out of him.

Jonah frowned. "But who will do my laundry if you run away?"

"Ha, ha, very funny," said an exasperated Calliope. So much for weaseling a compliment. She stomped a foot. "Now, move over. I'm hungry."

She brushed past Jonah into the pantry. She grabbed a box of Cheerios and sulked off to the windowed alcove off the kitchen that served as the dinette. After returning Mortimer to his cage, she sat on the narrow table wedged into the tight space.

Outside the window she heard the singsong chirping of a chickadee perched on Mom's bird feeder. Strange, but this morning the chickadee seemed to be singing for Calliope. "Your knees are knobby," she sang to herself in time to the chirping, "and your skating a bit wobbly."

If only it were true that someone was outside her window singing out her name in rhyme. She sighed and pitched one Cheerio at a time into her mouth. They tasted as stale as cardboard, but she kept tossing them down her gullet.

"What," said Jonah, standing at the opposite end of the dinette table, "no orange juice?"

Calliope looked down at her bowl of dry cereal. Oops, she'd indeed forgotten the signature ingredient, which made her Cheerios different from and better than anyone else's.

"Our baby sister is acting awfully strange this morning," mused Jonah.

"And I bet I know why," said Frederick. He clomped into the dinette, carrying the frying pan by its handle, which was draped in a towel. He sat down in front of the standing Jonah. From the head of the narrow table he grinned wolfishly down at Calliope.

Calliope figured he was up to something but she ignored him. She'd had her fill of teenage brothers this morning.

Jonah, however, took Frederick's bait. "What do you mean?"

"I mean," said Frederick between heaping forkfuls of egg, "she's fallen in love."

"Get out," said Jonah.

"I have proof."

Calliope turned sharply to face Frederick. She watched as his greasy fingers pulled a red piece of paper out of a top pocket of his army jacket. The poem—Calliope gasped. It must have fallen out of her pocket in the pantry. Now he'd taken it.

"Thief!" she screeched, jumping to her feet.

Smiling, Frederick waved the poem like a red flag.

It was impossible to move quickly on foot in the narrow dinette—and Frederick knew that. But Calliope bet he never figured she'd belly flop onto the table and slide across it into his face, which was what she did.

A surprised Frederick fell back against Jonah. But he didn't lose his grip on the poem. Instead his arm shot up, raising the poem out of Calliope's reach.

But Jonah succeeded where Calliope had failed. He plucked the note out of Frederick's fingertips and stepped back. Without Jonah to lean on, Frederick fell to the floor. For once he looked stunned.

"Thanks," Calliope wheezed to Jonah, but then realized she'd spoken too soon.

Jonah had no intention of returning the poem. He unfolded the red paper and began to read. "Not bad, not bad at all," he pronounced. "This boy is quite the poet."

"Who's a poet?" said Mom. She breezed into the dinette, her cell phone pressed against an ear and a breakfast bar sticking out of her mouth.

"Calliope's lover," said Jonah.

Mom spit out the breakfast bar. "What!"

"Here, see for yourself," said Jonah, turning to hand the poem to Mom.

At the sight of the red paper, Mom's eyes flashed as if she recognized it from upstairs.

Would she put two and two together? Calliope wasn't waiting to find out. She jumped up off the table and landed feet first on Frederick's stomach. He had been trying to sit up but her feet slammed him back down on the floor with a loud *oof.*

Using Frederick's muscular stomach as a springboard, Calliope bounced up, arm outstretched, and seized the paper from Jonah.

"Goodness," said Mom, recoiling in surprise.

Poem in hand, Calliope dashed through the kitchen and into the living room.

"Calliope!" she heard her mom call out from behind, but she didn't stop. "Sorry," she called back, "gotta go or I'll be late for school." And with that, Calliope ran out the door, three-headed charm tinkling in her wake.

Trolling for Poets

Calliope knew her neighborhood the way you knew your favorite song—by heart. Ear cocked, she awaited the opening refrain. There it was, the *swoosh, swoosh, swoosh* of a broom. It was wielded by Mrs. Blatherhorn, who was sweeping her already spotless front steps.

Friend and next-door neighbor Mrs. Blatherhorn—or Mrs. B., as Calliope loved to call her—watched Calliope after school until her mom returned home from work. Mrs. B.'s stern face brightened as she noticed Calliope, and she waved good morning.

Mrs. B.'s smile fell at the sound of a loud bang. She turned sharply to frown at a long wing-tipped car rumbling down the driveway next door. It was Mr. Oglemeyer off to work in his rusting Ford Fairlane. The Fairlane's tailpipe belched black smoke and again exploded. Its bang echoed off the small houses that sat shoulder to shoulder across the narrow street.

Calliope laughed and waved good-bye to the frowning Mrs. B. Soon Calliope came to Pizza Park, so named by her for its wedge shape, like a slice of pizza.

It was black-dirt pizza topped with matted brown grass and stones.

On the other side of the park the houses tripled in size. Most were made of wood, with high steps and banistered verandas. Many of the houses gleamed with purple, red and yellow gingerbread trimming.

Did Calliope's mystery poet live in one of these beautiful houses? It was fun to think he might. She'd never been inside one.

Calliope bounced her backpack so that her charm jingled loudly. She thought of Frederick trolling his plastic worm along the cattails of Sumner's Pond. Would her bait lure the mystery poet? At the moment all she was snaring were some cats, which prowled atop the banisters and meowed.

In the middle of the neighborhood of big wooden houses sat Calliope's school. A low building of sooty brick, it was fenced off from the surrounding homes. The school looked like a hobo who'd wandered into the wrong neighborhood and fallen asleep in a backyard.

Calliope's route led her to the rear of the school, where she was pretty much alone. Most kids either rode buses, which emptied out at the front of the school, or walked up the front sidewalk into the main lobby.

Not Calliope. She liked sneaking up on school. There was no entrance here on the rear of the school. You had to hop a low fence to enter the schoolyard.

One reason Calliope liked this route was that she'd found a secret clubhouse of sorts. Beneath a lone sycamore tree stood a rickety old picnic table. In the spring you could sit half-hidden behind the sycamore's low branches. Calliope loved to sit there and watch kids stream into school from behind the leafy veil.

In winter, of course, there was no veil to hide the table. Anyone could see it, if they paid attention. But luckily nobody but Calliope ever did. That is, until today. Now someone *else* had discovered her secret hiding place.

Nice Pair of Heads

What was Kevin doing crouched face first in the dirt under Calliope's table?

"Hey!" barked Calliope, sounding as miffed as she felt.

Kevin jumped, banging his head on the table's underside.

"Ouch." Calliope winced. Kevin said nothing, although he looked like he sorely wanted to rub his bruised head. Instead he crawled out from under the table, careful to keep his hands cupped together. He stood up in front of Calliope but stared down at his frayed brown low-top sneakers.

At first neither Calliope nor Kevin said a word. They didn't have to. Their clothing spoke for them. Calliope's pink sweatshirt answered "Whatever" to the "Proud to be a Nerd" written across Kevin's chest.

After a long moment, Kevin extended his cupped hands toward Calliope and unfolded them like a butterfly's wings.

Calliope couldn't believe what lay in Kevin's palms. It was the biggest, orangest beetle she had ever seen. The thing had jaws like the teeth of a staple remover. Could such a monstrously glorious bug really live in New Jersey? Calliope hoped not—especially if it hung out around her picnic table, of all places.

"It's quite rare, you know," said Kevin.

Thank goodness, thought Calliope.

"Would you like to hold it?" Kevin asked as if offering her a kitten.

"Ah . . . no thanks."

Still, she couldn't take her eyes off the thing. There was something fishy about it, if you could say that about a beetle. It rested in Kevin's hand like a rock. You'd think it would want to fly away but not a leg twitched. "Is it alive?"

"Sure. It's just . . . just resting."

"Resting? Like a stone, you mean."

"No, really. Look." Kevin tapped the beetle's rear and it inched across his hand without twitching a leg.

Calliope raised an eyebrow.

"So you don't want to touch it?" said Kevin, sounding disappointed.

Calliope crossed her arms, securing a hand under each armpit.

With a sigh Kevin slipped the beetle into a pocket. But there was no hiding those fierce jaws, which pressed out menacingly from his pants. Either Kevin had tamed that beetle like a dog or it was stone dead, thought Calliope.

But if the beetle were stone dead, why would Kevin carry it around? What a strange boy, thought

Calliope, turning to head toward the school. As she turned, her charm tinkled.

"What's that?" said Kevin.

Calliope stopped. "You mean this?" Again she wiggled the charm.

"Wow, did you make that?" said Kevin, pointing at the dangling heads.

"Uh-huh," said Calliope, shaking the heads.

"I didn't know girls liked to pinch off Barbie heads," Kevin said.

"Well, I'm not just any girl."

Kevin slipped a finger into a coil of his hair and began twisting it hard, as if trying to figure out what kind of girl *would* pinch off Barbie heads.

"Want to touch it?" said Calliope, unclipping the charm and holding it out toward Kevin. He hung back.

"Go on," said Calliope, "they won't bite."

Slowly Kevin reached for the charm. When his fingers touched the braid, Calliope loudly chomped her teeth.

Kevin recoiled.

"Sorry," giggled Calliope. Again she offered the charm to Kevin, but he kept his distance this time. "Oh, come on," she said. She really wanted a boy's opinion of her handiwork, and timid little Kevin was the only one handy.

She tossed the charm to him. He stepped back and the heads landed at his feet. In the dirt the charm must have looked less threatening. He squatted,

whatever

studying it now. Running an index finger along the heart-shaped knot, he murmured, "It's so . . . so . . ."

"Beautiful?" offered Calliope.

"Intricate—like a helix."

"A heal-what?"

"A helix," repeated Kevin, drawing a spiral in the air with his finger. "You know, a coil."

Kevin sure was smart. Was he sneaky, too? He *had* managed to creep unnoticed into Calliope's hiding place. She pictured him soundlessly slipping a red note onto the lip of Noreen's ice cream bowl and then fading back unnoticed into the dark rink.

"Ke-vin?" Calliope called playfully.

"Huh?" Kevin answered without looking up. He'd begun unraveling the knot as if to understand how it had been tied.

"Have you been following me?"

Kevin looked up sharply. "What?"

"You heard me."

Kevin's eyes shifted back to studying his frayed sneakers. Rising, he mumbled, "I told you. I was chasing that beetle."

"Uh-huh," said Calliope, sounding unconvinced.

Just then the first school bell rang. "Oh, gosh," said Kevin, "I forgot all about Mrs. Perkins. I promised to help her start up the class computers this morning." He dashed off toward the school, the beetle jouncing in his pocket.

Calliope scooped up her dusty charm and studied the half-tied knot of hair. Had she unraveled the mystery of the ice cream poet?

"Rod" Is Not a Car Part

As she dangled upside down from a high bar, Calliope's head buzzed as if hornets had nested between her ears. But questions tormented her, not hornets. Should she surrender the red note to Noreen, even though she hadn't yet found the mystery author? Or *had* she found him? And if she had, should she tell Noreen that Kevin liked her?

"You're awful quiet down there," said Noreen.

Calliope looked up at Noreen. It was recess and the two girls occupied a lone high bar at the back of the school playground. Ankles crossed, Noreen sat upright with her back against a wooden supporting beam.

"Noreen, do you like Kevin?"

"You mean the brain wonder?"

"Yeah."

Noreen raised her nose ever so slightly and considered Calliope's question. "He's kind of quiet, but I guess he's all right."

"But you don't *like* him, like him?"

Noreen's face pinched in concentration. Then she blushed and pointed a finger down at Calliope.

"You like him, don't you!"

"What?"

"I knew it! *That* explains the nutty outfit."

Calliope crossed her arms and pouted.

"Don't look so mad," said Noreen. "It happens to most girls eventually."

"What happens?" Calliope asked suspiciously.

"Falling in love."

"I'm not falling in love!"

Calliope began swaying back and forth, gathering momentum to swing back on top of the bar. She needed to straighten out Noreen right this minute. But she stopped in midswing. Something had slipped out of her pocket. She looked down to see her heads staring up at her from the worn grass below.

"Ooh, what's that?" Noreen called from above.

"That," said Calliope, unhooking her legs and falling into the dirt, "is my charm." She was happy to change the subject. "What do you think?" Calliope handed the dusty heads up to Noreen.

"It's different, I'll give you that," said Noreen, dangling the charm in front of her. "Is this why Kevin likes you?"

"Noreen, I told you . . ." Calliope stopped as she saw Noreen's gaze shift to something over her shoulder. Calliope turned to see a boy standing behind her in a grease-spotted tweed jacket and a frayed, lopsided bow tie.

"Oh, hello . . . Rod," she said, pronouncing the short name as hard as the metal cylinder inside any car. Calliope knew he hated to be called that. He preferred the grander Rodney.

Rodney ignored Calliope. "Did you make that?" he asked Noreen, pointing up at the heads dangling from her fingertips. He sounded impressed. Was he trying to make up for tormenting them at the rink?

Noreen acted miffed, as if she hadn't forgotten. Calliope knew better. Rodney's attack at Spackle's was long since forgotten. What, then, was Noreen up to, ignoring Rodney for a long moment? When she finally spoke, it wasn't to answer no. But neither did she say yes. What she said was "Do you like them?" Then she tinkled the heads for Rodney.

"Hmm," said Rodney, offering up an open palm. "May I?"

Noreen shrugged and dropped the heads into Rodney's hand.

Rodney nodded approvingly as he examined the heart-shaped knot of the charm.

"Pretty neat, huh?" said Noreen.

"You bet," said Rodney, beaming up at her.

"Oh, I didn't make it," said Noreen.

"No?"

"It belongs to Calliope."

"Really?" said Rodney.

"Yeah," said Calliope, crossing her arms and glaring at Rodney. Ha! Now he'd have to compliment her, something he'd never done before.

Nor would he do it now. His fingers curled around the charm. Then he cocked back his arm and hurled the charm over Calliope's head.

"Hey!" cried Calliope as she watched her charm

sail high and far, finally plummeting into a thicket of rhododendrons bordering the playground.

Calliope shoved the smirking Rodney aside and sprinted off to retrieve her charm. When she was halfway down the playground the school bell rang, signaling the end of recess.

No sooner had the bell rung than a towering woman with a pencil-thin smile stepped in front of Calliope, stopping her cold. It was Mrs. Sterne, the principal. "B-b-but," sputtered Calliope, pointing toward the thicket.

"No buts," said Mrs. Sterne. "Recess is over." She spun Calliope around and shooed her toward the line of kids entering the school. Calliope glanced over her shoulder. She'd get her charm back—no matter what.

Cat and Mouse

"Really, your charm wasn't *that* great," said Noreen.

"It was to me," grumped a pouting Calliope.

The girls sat side by side in a classroom where desks were clustered in groups of four.

"Why did you have to tease Rodney?" nagged Calliope.

Noreen smiled faintly.

"You're not turning into Ashley, are you?"

Noreen ignored the question and instead began chanting, "Calliope and Kevin, sitting in a tree . . ."

"Don't start that again!" Calliope turned away sharply, giving Noreen the back of her head. Noreen's ponytail whipped the back of Calliope's head as she too turned away.

Fine, be that way, thought Calliope. She looked up front, waiting for Mrs. Perkins to resume class. The teacher sat atop a high stool in front of the chalkboard, surveying the kids drifting back into her classroom. Most milled about their desks until Mrs. Perkins suddenly clapped three times. The sharp sound broke like thunder over the students and they scrambled to their seats.

Mrs. Perkins clearly wanted to begin, sitting with an open history book in her lap. But someone wouldn't let her.

Rodney stood, bow tie askew, holding a pink flower with big petals that flopped like a beagle's ears. He offered the showy flower to Mrs. Perkins.

At first Mrs. Perkins tried to ignore Rodney by looking hard at the book in her lap and loudly flipping the pages. If that was a signal for Rodney to take his seat, he didn't get it. He just stood there, inching his flower closer and closer to Mrs. Perkins's nose.

With a sigh of resignation, Mrs. Perkins finally looked up at the flower. She looked weary. Calliope didn't blame her. Mrs. Perkins had a drawerful of gifts from Rodney.

Calliope watched as a curious standoff began. Mrs. Perkins wouldn't take the flower but Rodney still held it out to her. He stood, beaming, like a dog awaiting a pat on the head for bringing in the newspaper.

Mrs. Perkins finally caved in. "Why, thank you," she said, snatching the flower out of Rodney's hand, and nodded toward his chair.

Rodney meandered, savoring his triumph, through the desks to his seat. He sat next to Kevin in the cluster of desks just in front of Calliope and Noreen.

Kevin already had his notebook open. He was famous for his dog-eared and ever-present notebooks. Kevin took down Mrs. Perkins's every word. No wonder he was the best student in the class. Maybe even in the whole fourth grade.

Mrs. PerKins

Kevin sat now, hand poised with pen above the page. When Mrs. Perkins began to speak, his hand hit the paper with a furious scrawl.

Rodney, on the other hand, had no notebook. Nor did he seem to be listening to Mrs. Perkins. Instead he was poking his head over Kevin's shoulder to see what Kevin was writing.

Without looking up, Kevin raised his shoulder to block Rodney's view. Undeterred, Rodney leaned forward to see around the raised shoulder. Kevin hunched forward and Rodney leaned sideways. Rodney kept shifting. Poor Kevin was twisting himself into knots trying to shield his notebook from Rodney's prying eyes.

Calliope tried hard to follow Mrs. Perkins's story about how Columbus thought he'd discovered a new continent, when it was really only the island of Hispaniola. Really she did. But her attention kept drifting back to the seesawing boys in front of her.

How different yet alike they were, thought Calliope. Each wanted Mrs. Perkins's approval. But Rodney tried to win it with gifts and flattery, while Kevin used good grades and a helping hand.

Was one of them the mystery poet? Calliope considered the evidence. Did Rodney like Noreen? He had been hanging around her lately but Calliope had never seen him with either pen or book in hand outside class.

Kevin, on the other hand, could be found most summer afternoons in the town library, nestled in a beanbag chair with a book.

Calliope watched Kevin now, hand racing across his notebook as Mrs. Perkins talked. He seemed more secretary than poet.

Neither Rodney nor Kevin seemed much like Calliope's dad. Her dad had read a lot but mostly in the bathroom, where he kept a stack of half-finished books. He'd use bits of what he'd read—a funny name or line—to make you laugh. No, Dad didn't need wilting pink flowers to make you like him. Humor was his gift.

Calliope sighed. Her search must go on. And for that she'd need her three-headed charm. Just wait till she got her hands on it again. With wagging finger she'd scold, "This time you'd better scare up the right boy."

Missing Heads

Where were the heads?

Calliope lay belly down, again pawing the dirt under the thicket of rhododendrons at the back of the schoolyard. Nothing. She rolled over onto her back and peered up through the leathery evergreen leaves. No sign of her Barbie heads there, either.

It made no sense. She and Noreen had been alone when Rodney had tossed Calliope's heads into the shrubs. Puzzled, Calliope wiggled out from under the bushes. It was then that she saw the showy pink flowers budding on the back of the bush. It was unusual to see bushes bloom in late March but the weather had been awfully warm the past few days.

Calliope hadn't been the only one to notice the blooming rhododendrons. "Rodney," she muttered. He must have found the heads while picking a flower for Mrs. Perkins. But how had he gotten around Mrs. Sterne in the first place? Easy, Calliope now realized. The principal had been preoccupied with shooing Calliope back to class.

"Oh no you don't!" sputtered Calliope, jumping to her feet. She set off to pay Rodney a visit.

Rodney never talked about home but Calliope knew where he lived. She'd once seen him peering out of a large window on the second floor of a brick building. The building served as the office of Spanoli & Sons Auto Fix-it Shop. Rodney's last name was Spanoli. It was no more than three blocks from her house.

Calliope stood now in front of the little brick building. She looked up at the second-story window, but the curtains were drawn. She didn't see anyone inside the office. No matter. Calliope let herself inside. Bells jingled overhead as she entered, but no one appeared at the worn front counter.

"Hello?" When no one answered, Calliope walked around the counter and through a swinging door that opened into the garage itself.

The cavernous garage was empty except for an aging red convertible. Two pairs of denim-clad legs in black boots protruded from under the car.

Calliope walked up to the longer pair of blue legs and squatted, craning her neck sideways to peer under the convertible. Underneath was a figure lying faceup on a small cart. "Hello?"

This time her call was heeded. The sound of squeaking wheels echoed in the garage as a man rolled out from under the convertible. He stared at Calliope a moment, knitting up his grease-stained eyebrows. Then he beamed at her with a mouthful of yellow teeth. "You're Frederick's little sister?"

"Yes, sir," answered Calliope. "Are you Mr. Spanoli, Rodney's dad?"

Mr. Spanoli nodded and then called out, "Hey, Duane, it's Frederick Day's little sister."

The other set of blue legs rolled out from under the car, revealing a boy who looked strikingly like Rodney, except he was tall, bearded and wore a grease-stained T-shirt. Duane also flashed a mouthful of yellow teeth at Calliope.

"Well, how's that car doing?" said Mr. Spanoli.

"My mom's Saturn?"

Mr. Spanoli laughed. "Not that boring old thing. The Camaro!"

Calliope remembered now that Frederick had won the car in a poker game. He and some friends had rolled it down the street to this garage, where Mr. Spanoli had resurrected it in a day. In a hushed voice Frederick had pronounced Mr. Spanoli's hands gifted, as if he were a famous surgeon.

"The Musclemobile is fine, I guess," said Calliope, picturing Frederick's car sagging against the curb outside her house.

"Don't tell me you have a car that I need to look at," said Mr. Spanoli, chuckling at his own joke.

"Me? No, sir. I've come to see Rodney."

"Who?"

"Rod."

"Oh, him I know." Mr. Spanoli also preferred the shorter, metallic-sounding Rod—but not as an insult. He studied Calliope's "Whatever" sweatshirt and baggy balloon pants.

"Is he home?" Calliope asked.

"He's upstairs," said Mr. Spanoli, nodding toward the ceiling, "hiding."

"From me?"

"I don't think so," said Mr. Spanoli with a laugh, "although he's never had a girl visitor before. Especially one so, ah, dressed up."

Calliope blushed as Rodney's father beamed at her.

"May I see him?" Calliope asked.

"I don't see why not. Take the stairs behind the front desk."

Dust Balls and Dirty Dishes

Calliope found a small apartment at the top of the stairs. She stood in a room that was both the kitchen and the living room, with windows looking out onto the street. A pile of unwashed dishes towered high in the sink. If those dishes had been in her sink, Mom would have blown a gasket, as Frederick would say. Nor would her mom have cared for the dust balls swirling across the wooden floors like tumbleweeds. And Mom would have paled at the sight of the grimy green couch and matching chair under the window. Calliope's furniture was frayed too, but it was clean.

Ugly furniture. Dust balls. Unwashed dishes in the sink. All this grime seemed to be telling her something, like a message scrawled on a dirty windshield. As Calliope's eyes swept the apartment she realized the message lay in what was missing. There wasn't a single picture of Rodney's mother—either with him or his father. There were lots of pictures of Calliope's father at her house. If Rodney's mother had died she imagined they would have pictures of her, too.

Rodney's parents must be divorced. And it must have been a bad one. It was as if she'd never existed.

Any trace of her had been erased. Air whistled through Calliope's teeth like a cooling radiator venting steam. It was going to be darn hard to hate Rodney now.

Calliope remembered that first year after her father's death. Woe to anyone who mentioned his name or reminded Calliope of Dad. Such a person was sure to receive a kick in the shin, courtesy of Calliope. That went double for boys. And it took a while before she could look at his picture.

Did Calliope somehow remind Rodney of his mother? Maybe she had blond hair, was adventurous or collected Barbie heads. Was that why he had always been so mean to Calliope?

Well, if so, Calliope knew how to take care of that! She'd draw out Rodney's meanness like pus from an infected cut. That was what Mom had done to her. She'd made Calliope talk and talk about Dad. How much she missed him; how unfair it was that he'd had to die. And it *was* unfair, darn unfair.

Talking didn't end the pain. But it did turn the pain into something she could handle, sort of like a difficult brother you could learn to live with. She'd been through it. Now she could show Rodney how to live with his loss.

But first she had to find him. She called out his name, but he didn't answer. Still, she didn't give up. She walked down a hallway leading off the main room. There were two doors opposite each other at the end of the hall. One door had a knob blackened with grease; the other shone grease-free. That was the door Calliope knocked on. "Rodney?"

No one answered, but Calliope heard what sounded like a mouse scrambling for the safety of its hole. She turned the knob and the unlocked door opened. She stepped inside to find a room that looked like it belonged in another house.

Clean would be too dirty a word for this room. There were no swirling dust balls or grimy slippers. The room's sole decoration was a cloth replica of a dollar bill. It hung flaglike above a tall metallic bookshelf. Beneath the flag sat a transparent plastic piggy bank bursting with coins.

Calliope inched toward the shelf, eyes peeled for a leaping Rodney. He could be like a panther, hidden and watching, ready to pounce at the most embarrassing moment.

At the bookless shelf she picked up a magazine from one of the many stacks of them. "*Young Entrepreneur.*" She read the magazine title aloud softly. The word *entrepreneur* buzzed in her nose, so she figured it must be French.

But she didn't need the French-speaking Noreen to figure out what the word meant. The magazine's cover with a boy in sport coat and bow tie brandishing a fistful of dollar bills gave it away.

Boy, Rodney sure had money on the brain. So did Calliope's mom, but this was different. Mom worried about having enough money to pay the bills. Rodney seemed interested in having more than enough.

In that way Rodney was sort of like Noreen, with her red Mercedes and towering house. Except Noreen never thought about money. Not even when she forgot to bring some to school to buy an ice cream at lunch. She assumed someone would buy it for her and Calliope always did.

Rodney was turning out to be more fascinating than she'd ever imagined. Motherless, obsessed with money and a suck-up. What would Calliope discover next about him? He'd always been like a book she'd never bothered to read beyond the first couple of pages. Now she wanted to devour his whole story.

Calliope put *Young Entrepreneur* back and picked up a magazine from another stack. This one she recognized immediately. It was *House Magnificent,* which Mom leafed through while waiting in line at the supermarket.

What would a boy be doing with *House Magnificent*? She began to flip through it and stopped at a glossy photograph spread across two pages. In the picture a willowy woman and her daughter sat in high-backed wooden chairs in a cavernous room with a marble floor. Each sipped from a flowered teacup, pinkies raised.

Calliope would recognize those raised pinkies anywhere. They belonged to Noreen and her mother, Mrs. Catherwood.

Oh ho ho. Wait till she told Noreen that Rodney kept a magazine photo of her by his nightstand. What would Noreen say—would she even believe Calliope?

As Calliope pondered these questions, she heard a creaking sound and froze.

The Boy in the Basket

Calliope cringed in anticipation. But there was no pounce, no shout of "Aha!" just the creaking. Her eye fell on a waist-high wicker basket at the foot of Rodney's bed. She hadn't paid much attention to the basket before, but she studied it now. The foot of the basket bulged like a python that had just swallowed a pony—or maybe a nine-year-old boy.

Calliope set down *House Magnificent* and tiptoed over to the basket. Silently she raised the lid.

At first nothing looked out of the ordinary. Then she noticed that the dirty socks and underwear piled high in the basket inched up and down like a pair of breathing lungs. And wasn't that a tweedy elbow poking through a pair of boxer shorts?

Suddenly the laundry spoke. "Dad, please. I don't want to learn how to clean the carburetor."

So that was what Rodney's father had meant. His son was hiding from him! He didn't want to help out in the garage.

Oh, dear. Calliope felt her resolve to be good to Rodney wilt like the talking underwear she eyed. It wasn't every day you got a chance to embarrass Rodney and she couldn't bring herself to fritter it away.

"I don't know," she said from deep in her throat, trying to imitate the voice of Mr. Spanoli.

The laundry didn't respond for a moment. Then it asked weakly, "Dad?"

"Guess again," said Calliope.

She watched as Rodney's head rose slowly out of the laundry. His normally ruddy face blanched as white as the underwear hanging off his ear. He sputtered, but no recognizable words came out.

Rodney looked thoroughly flummoxed and Calliope felt his embarrassment. She'd gone too far and her conscience let her know it, throbbing like a stubbed toe. She scrambled to apologize, if only indirectly.

"I—I—I just came over to say that if you really want to keep my Barbie heads, they're yours. Honest."

That said, she just wanted to go home. She scurried toward the bedroom door but stopped in the doorway at the sound of a loud *splat* against the hardwood floor. She glanced over her shoulder. Rodney was lying with cheek smooshed against the floor amid a pile of dirty clothes. He must have toppled the wicker basket trying to climb out.

"No... wait," he mumbled through a scrunched mouth.

He sounded neither angry nor embarrassed, which struck Calliope as odd. If she'd been sprawled facedown on the floor her tongue would have been

whatever

knotted with embarrassment. Against her better judgment, she stopped.

Rodney slithered out of the basket and rose to his feet. Righting the basket, he stuffed the clothes back inside. Then he straightened his lopsided bow tie. All in all, he acted as if tumbling out of a laundry hamper were a perfectly normal thing to do.

It was an amazing performance, thought Calliope.

"These heads," Rodney said to Calliope, "are they the ones I threw into the bushes at school?"

"Yes," said Calliope, "but—"

He raised the palm of his hand to stop her from speaking further.

"I'm sorry," he said.

"You're what?" Calliope wasn't sure she'd heard right.

"I said I'm sorry. I shouldn't have thrown your Barbie heads into the bushes."

Had Rodney knocked himself silly tumbling out of the basket? He'd never apologized to Calliope before. Not even when he had wiped his hands, sticky with fresh blue finger paint, on her new white T-shirt in second grade.

"Soda?" asked Rodney.

"Sure," croaked Calliope. Her throat had gone dry. Was it from shock?

Rodney guided Calliope to the edge of his bed to sit. "I'll be back in a jiffy," he said, then left the bedroom.

Calliope sat obediently, dazed by Rodney's unexpected friendliness. Still, a faint voice in the back of her head wondered, What is he up to?

The Luckiest Girl

True to his word, Rodney returned in a jiffy, a can of 7UP in each hand. It was Noreen's favorite soda, not Calliope's, but she accepted it from him all the same.

Rodney pulled up a footstool and sat at Calliope's feet. Was he trying to make her feel important? If so, he was doing a good job.

Calliope popped open her 7UP and raised the can up to her nose. The spritzing soda tickled her nostrils, working like smelling salts to revive her from her daze. This soda, she now wondered, was it not like the flower Rodney had given Mrs. Perkins? Was Rodney trying to flatter her?

Calliope couldn't think of anything she had that Rodney might want. There were only a few coins in her piggy bank.

But there was something she wanted from Rodney. She was dying to find out the truth about his mother. And, if he'd let her, to comfort him, just a little.

She sipped the 7UP. The icy soda watered her dry throat and she regained her voice. "So," she ventured cautiously, "do you live alone with your dad?"

Rodney's head twitched as if shaking off the question. Calliope tried again: "I used to stay home alone after school."

Rodney finally spoke, although not about his family. "I'm so sorry but I don't have your heads."

If Rodney was trying to stop Calliope from asking about his mother, he succeeded. "What do you mean?"

"I mean, somebody else must have taken your heads."

Calliope studied Rodney's face, deciding whether to believe him. Normally she wouldn't have but he was being so nice. If he hadn't taken her charm, then who had? It was all very puzzling.

Rodney seemed bent on confusing her even more. "You know," he said, looking adoringly up at her, "you're the luckiest kid in school."

"How's that?" she asked. She had tried to feign indifference but her voice betrayed her keen interest.

"You're best friends with the richest girl in school," Rodney answered.

Aha, thought Calliope, now Rodney's showing his hand. The apology. The soda. The politeness. It was all about "Noreen, my Noreen." He sure had a thing for her. But could Rodney really be the mystery poet? Calliope surveyed his room again. Not only weren't there any books, there wasn't any paper or a typewriter in sight.

Calliope's eyes drifted back down to the boy sitting at her feet.

"I bet you know more about Noreen than anyone else." Rodney looked up at Calliope with pleading puppy-dog eyes.

Calliope couldn't resist. "Did you know that Noreen rides home every day in a big red Mercedes?"

"No!"

Calliope nodded. "And her house is like... like..."

"Buckingham Palace?"

That's how the magazine had described Noreen's house but Calliope knew better. "Well, not exactly."

"What do you mean?" said Rodney, sounding a shade less friendly than before.

"It's hard to explain unless you've seen Noreen's house for yourself."

"Are you saying you've been inside?" scoffed Rodney.

"Are you kidding? Lots of times."

Rodney leaned back, folding his arms with a look that said, Yeah, right.

"Well, I have."

"Uh-huh."

So much for playing Mr. Oh-I'm-so-sorry. Rodney had reverted to his old maddening self. Well, Calliope would show him. "I've had tea and cookies with Noreen *and* her mom."

"You just read that in the magazine."

"That's not true," Calliope shot back.

Rodney looked unimpressed.

Calliope glared down at him and considered

kicking over his little stool. Then she had a better idea. "How would you like to see Noreen's house for yourself?"

"Who's going to take me—you?" Rodney asked with a small laugh.

"Exactly."

"Yeah, right."

"You'll see. I'll get Noreen to invite you home and then won't you feel stupid."

No sooner had Calliope challenged Rodney than *she* began to feel like the stupid one. Why, she wasn't exactly sure. But she suspected it had something to do with Rodney grinning as if he'd just won the lottery.

How Could You?

"How could you?" Noreen whispered harshly to Calliope, who sat alongside her in the back of the red Mercedes.

Calliope shrugged. What could she say? She'd rather eat brussels sprouts for a month than admit the truth, which was that Rodney had tricked her. Now she'd entrapped Noreen into inviting Rodney home.

The trap had been surprisingly easy to set. Noreen and Calliope were short one member of the team required for their science project. So Calliope had suggested to Mrs. Perkins that she add Rodney to their team. Noreen had stomped her shiny black leather shoe in protest but Mrs. Perkins loved the idea. "Maybe you girls can get Rodney to take his homework seriously," Mrs. Perkins had challenged.

Noreen could never say no to a teacher.

It had been a victory, all right, but a costly one for Calliope. The harshly whispered question was the only thing Noreen had said to Calliope since her chauffeur, Charles, had picked them up after school. As the Mercedes purred toward her house, Noreen stared straight ahead, arms crossed. She didn't even offer Calliope an icy soda out of the little fridge hidden under the backseat's armrest.

Calliope sighed, fingering the white plastic garbage bag nestled between her legs. It bulged with empty cans, milk cartons, newspapers and cardboard tubes—all of which they had to fashion somehow into a working invention for Mrs. Perkins. This junk was Calliope's contribution to the science project. Noreen was providing her house as their laboratory. What would Rodney add—other than serving as a wedge between Calliope and Noreen?

Calliope glanced up front at Rodney, who was busy buttering up Charles.

"You handle this Mercedes like a fighter pilot dodging a barrage of enemy fire," oozed Rodney.

Calliope thought she might be sick—and it wasn't from the motion of the car. Luckily she wasn't alone.

"Hey," Noreen barked at Rodney, "don't bother Charles while he's driving."

"It's quite all right, miss," Charles assured her.

Noreen glowered at Calliope.

Geez, thought Calliope with a cringe, she couldn't wait for this afternoon to end. Then she'd be free of Rodney and the horrible boast she'd made to him. Never again would she let someone goad her into bragging. For now, though, she was just as trapped as Noreen. They would both have to endure an afternoon of Rodney.

Thank goodness the Mercedes was soon pulling

in to the circular brick driveway of Noreen's house. The car had barely stopped before Rodney popped out.

That was a big no-no. You were supposed to wait until Charles unlocked the doors and let everyone out, one by one.

Though first out of the car Rodney hadn't gone anywhere. He stood with his head tilted back and a hand cupped to his brow, staring up at the soaring front wall of Noreen's house. "Wow," he whispered, "it *is* Buckingham Palace."

"No," corrected Calliope, slipping up behind Rodney, "this palace belongs to the Queen of Hearts."

"Huh?"

"You'll see," said Calliope. She slapped her lumpy garbage bag into his behind, trying to nudge him toward the house.

Noreen strode past Calliope and Rodney and disappeared through the arching doorway.

Someone was still peeved. No matter, thought Calliope. She'd make it up to Noreen later. Right now she had to keep a sharp eye on Rodney. Who knew what he'd do next? She lingered behind him, not letting him out of her sight.

He poked along, savoring every detail of the driveway, towering front bushes and heavy wooden front door. The eight-sided foyer stopped him cold. His eyes bulged at the sight of the white marble floor, each tile featuring a little red heart.

"See? I told you," said Calliope. "Now off with

those shoes." She pointed at Rodney's scuffed loafers. The only one allowed to wear shoes in Noreen's house was Mrs. Catherwood.

As they slid in their socks across the great foyer, Calliope enjoyed Rodney's awed silence. She knew it wouldn't last. Before long he'd open his big mouth again, this time to try to charm Mrs. Catherwood. Calliope wondered if he'd tucked away a showy pink flower for the occasion.

A lot of good it would do him. Mrs. Catherwood was no Mrs. Perkins. Imagine a spelling-bee judge who not only asked you to spell the hardest word in the dictionary but spell it backward as well. That was Mrs. Catherwood.

Mrs. Catherwood liked Calliope but in the way a queen enjoyed her court jester. What would she make of Rodney in his greasy tweed jacket and lopsided bow tie? Calliope savored the thought.

Queen of Hearts

Calliope found Noreen with her mother in what Calliope called the throne room. It was cavernous and empty, except for a centered oasis of ancient furniture. At the heart of this oasis sat a coffee table on an Oriental rug. On one side of the table were two wooden chairs and on the other a high-backed chair with crushed-velvet cushions.

In the high-backed chair sat Mrs. Catherwood, holding a flowered teacup in one hand with her pinky raised. The slender fingers of her other hand toyed with a pearl necklace as she inspected her daughter. Noreen sat across from her mother sipping tea, also with her pinky raised.

Calliope knew to stand under the high arch of the doorway, waiting to be recognized.

Not Rodney. He rushed into the room, planting himself between Noreen and her mother. "I want to thank you," he gushed, "for inviting me to your beautiful house."

Oh, boy, thought Calliope, Rodney had done it now. Nobody addressed Mrs. Catherwood until she addressed you first.

Mrs. Catherwood didn't reply, looking through Rodney to her daughter.

"Mother," said Noreen, lowering her teacup, "this is Rodney. He's come to help us with our science project."

Mrs. Catherwood's gaze drifted to Rodney. A faint smile crossed her lips as she eyed his jacket and bow tie.

"Mrs. Catherwood, may I ask you a question?" said Rodney.

Mrs. Catherwood signaled her consent with a slight nod.

"Is it true," Rodney began grandly, "that the rug I'm standing on once belonged to Suleiman the Magnificent?"

Oh, please. Calliope snorted. Rodney didn't know who was president of the United States, let alone anything about Suleiman the Whoever. He was either making this up . . . or had read it in *House Magnificent.* No matter. His little performance sounded phony.

Not so, apparently, to Mrs. Catherwood. She drew back, studying Rodney with a raised eyebrow. "Don't tell me you're familiar with the history of the great tapestry of the Ottoman Empire?"

Rodney smiled as if he knew all about it.

"Why, Noreen, what an impressive young man."

Geez, thought Calliope, Rodney could wring a smile out of a granite slab. Even hard-to-impress Noreen looked awed at how quickly Rodney had charmed her mother.

This had to stop—and now. Calliope rattled her bag of junk from the doorway. “Aren’t we forgetting something?”

Mrs. Catherwood glanced toward Calliope. “All right, you three,” she said, dismissing them with a wave of her hand. “Run along to your project. Don’t hesitate to call Louisa if you need anything.”

“Who’s Louisa?” Rodney whispered to Noreen as the three of them left the throne room.

“Our servant, of course.”

Rodney beamed.

Oh, brother, Calliope thought. She trailed behind Noreen and Rodney as they climbed the great winding staircase that led upstairs to Noreen’s bedroom.

Noreen’s bedroom was big and airy with lots of windows. Blond-wood bookshelves spanned the walls, brimming with the most fascinating knickknacks. There were earthen tea sets, lacquered boxes of all colors and dancing Buddhas carved out of stone and wood. Her father collected this stuff on his world travels and sold it to expensive stores in New York.

Noreen’s knickknacks drew Rodney like a pirate to buried treasure, but Calliope had seen it all many times before. She just wanted to get cracking on their project. She plopped down in the middle of Noreen’s carpeted floor and emptied her bag. Out poured soda cans, Popsicle sticks, fuzzy wires, coat hangers and milk cartons.

“Now,” she said, rubbing her hands together, “what should we make? A Ferris wheel? A space station? How about a left-handed smoke shifter?”

Calliope chuckled, thinking she'd made a pretty good joke. She looked up to see if Rodney or Noreen had thought so too.

Neither of them paid any attention to Calliope. They were too busy playing some kind of compliment game. Rodney circled the room, praising everything from Noreen's Buddhas to her high canopy bed.

Enough already, thought Calliope, eagerly waiting for Noreen to tell Rodney to knock it off. But she didn't.

Noreen stood erect at an end bookshelf, hand on hip and nose raised ever so slightly, issuing thank-you after thank-you.

At this rate, worried Calliope, they'd never get started on the science project. Which would mean Rodney would have to come back. Ha! Calliope bet that had been his plan all along.

Well, it wouldn't work. Calliope knew how to make Noreen forget all about Rodney and his sickening deluge of compliments.

A Poet Unmasked

Captain Tweakerbeak was the most interesting of all Noreen's exotic knickknacks. In a head no bigger than a jumbo gum ball, Captain Tweakerbeak had stuffed a vast library of human sound. Yet you couldn't play back any of it on command. The captain was like a CD player that had developed a mind of its own. One minute he'd coo "Darling, just darling" like Mrs. Catherwood, and the next moment he turned into Bugs Bunny asking Elmer Fudd "What's up, Doc?" You never knew what the captain would say next. Which made him more fun than Saturday-morning cartoons.

The captain was an African gray parrot who lived in a tall cage in a back corner of Noreen's room. There he sat perched on a swing, head cocked to focus one eye on a small television sitting atop a stool just outside his cage. The captain eyed Pepé Le Pew as he tried in vain to persuade Penelope the cat to love him.

Poor Pepé. He was a skunk who couldn't help raising a stink. Just like Noreen couldn't help that she was rich, nor could Calliope help that she liked to collect Barbie heads. That was just who they were. Could the mystery poet help wooing girls with rhyme, Calliope wondered?

Captain Tweakerbeak cocked his head to eye Calliope. "Ooh, *ma chérie,*" he cooed just like Pepé.

"Oh, stop," said Calliope, blushing. She opened the door to his cage and extended an arm toward the parrot. Up the captain climbed along Calliope's arm until he reached her shoulder. Then he nestled into the curve of her neck as if it were his favorite place. Calliope certainly hoped it was.

With the captain aboard, Calliope crept up behind Rodney.

"*Awk,*" said the captain, eyeing Rodney, "are you a good witch or a bad witch?" Glinda of *The Wizard of Oz* couldn't have said it better herself.

The sound of the captain's voice drew Noreen like a doting mother to her small child. She elbowed Rodney aside and began to scratch Captain Tweakerbeak under the neck. The captain threw back his head and gurgled loudly. "Captain, really," fussed Noreen, but she kept scratching despite her professed disapproval.

Calliope happily noted that Rodney now stood behind Noreen like yesterday's favored toy.

But unlike a toy, Rodney could speak. He renewed his flattery with a vengeance. "So many books," he gushed. "I bet you've read every one of them."

If Noreen had she wasn't saying.

Most boys would have sulked off under Noreen's

lack of interest. But not Rodney, observed Calliope. He just switched tactics. With a loud crunch he slid on his knees into the junk strewn across the floor. "Come on, guys," he said, picking up a milk carton, "we haven't got all afternoon."

Still Noreen ignored him. "Watch this," she said to Calliope, and began to rub her knuckles slowly and deeply into the captain's little gray skull.

"Ooh la la," cooed the captain.

Noreen cooed back, *"Je t'aime beaucoup,"* and nuzzled the captain's chest.

Calliope didn't need to speak a word of French to understand what was going on here. The captain had won the heart of his Penelope—and Rodney was none too happy about it. His face reddened with jealousy. Rodney glared at the captain for a long moment and then did a very odd thing, especially for a boy. Especially for a boy who didn't have a book in his room.

He began to recite poetry.

The poetry did the trick. Noreen turned to look down at Rodney.

He winked at Noreen as if confessing to some unsolved mystery between the two of them.

Noreen's brow wrinkled with confusion.

Of course Noreen had no idea what Rodney was referring to. How could she? Calliope had never shown Noreen the red note. But Calliope knew every word of it by heart. That was why she could do what she did next.

"When you're Noreen, my Noreen, you skate as

you please," interjected Calliope, finishing the poem for Rodney. "Noreen, my Noreen, would you skate with me, please?"

"Noreen, my Noreen?" muttered a befuddled Noreen. She turned to look at Calliope.

Calliope shrugged as if she'd done nothing more than recite any old nursery rhyme.

Noreen wasn't buying it. Her eyes narrowed like a tough cop preparing to grill a suspect.

Apology Not Accepted

Way to go, Mom!

Not only had Calliope's mother shown up on time, a first in and of itself, but she was even early. Her arrival at Noreen's had spared Calliope from a grueling cross-examination. When Louisa announced Mom, Calliope grabbed Rodney by the arm and dragged him sputtering out of the bedroom.

Now Calliope sat in the cramped backseat of Mom's car. She strained not to slide down the sagging seat into Rodney. Calliope had tried to climb up front but Mom had stopped her, insisting she ride in back to keep her guest company.

Some company. Rodney sat with his arms crossed, glaring out the window. Calliope crossed her arms too and tried to concentrate on the passing scenery. Her gaze, though, kept drifting back to the boy smoldering next to her. Could Rodney really have written the poem on the red note? It seemed so unlikely, yet how else would he know the words?

The mystery of it gnawed at Calliope. The more she thought about Rodney, the more he blossomed in her imagination. She pictured him hunkered over an old typewriter, typing poem after poem by candlelight in the middle of the night.

Calliope's tongue burned with questions and it would burst into flames if she stayed silent another moment. "Did you really write that poem about Noreen?" she asked Rodney.

Rodney didn't respond.

Undeterred, she tried harder. "It was really good, you know."

The compliment drew Rodney's head from the window but he still wouldn't look at Calliope, preferring instead to stare straight ahead.

"I mean it," pressed Calliope.

Rodney uncrossed his arms and looked down at the hands in his lap. "Do you really think so?"

She nodded.

"Can I ask you a question?" Rodney said, still studying his hands.

"Sure," she said brightly, thinking she'd finally won him over.

"How come you know the words of my poem and Noreen doesn't?" Rodney looked up at Calliope for the first time.

"Oh, that . . ."

Rodney's look hardened.

"Don't blame me," said Calliope. "You stuck your love note in the wrong ice cream."

"No I didn't."

"Well, you stuck the note in Noreen's ice cream while I was eating it."

"So you stole my poem?"

"Not exactly!"

"Then how come you never gave it to Noreen?"

He had her there. When Calliope didn't answer, Rodney recrossed his arms and again stared out the window.

Calliope glanced up to see Mom frowning at her in the rearview mirror, wondering, no doubt, why Rodney wasn't smiling. Which meant soon she'd be butting in, asking questions of her own, questions Calliope didn't want to answer.

But the truth was, Calliope didn't want Rodney angry at her, either. She wanted him to confide all about his secret life as a poet.

Why did Rodney write—and why to Noreen? Was it that she—not Calliope—somehow reminded him of his mom? Or did he really love her? Calliope wanted answers but she knew there was only one way now to win over Rodney, and it wasn't pleasant. "I'm sorry, okay?"

Without turning from the window, Rodney said, "Apology not accepted."

"What?" cried Calliope.

"You heard me."

"Oh, come on."

"All right," said Rodney, turning again to face her, "but only on one condition."

"What's that?" she asked warily.

"You give my poem to Noreen."

"Fair enough," said Calliope, relieved.

"And tell her what a great guy I am."

"Now, wait a minute," protested Calliope. "That's two conditions."

"Math was never my best subject."

"What is?" sneered Calliope.

"Is everything all right back there?" Mom called out.

"Yes, Mom," Calliope chirped. Then she leaned toward Rodney and said through her teeth, "Oh, all right."

Rodney relaxed against the seat for the first time.

What a maddening boy, thought Calliope. But she had to give him credit. Rodney was a clever rascal. Her brother Frederick would have just pounded her into submission. Not Rodney. He never clenched a fist. All the same she felt as if he'd twisted her up like a stick of licorice.

All right. Calliope would do Rodney's bidding. But she wanted something in return, like answers to some of her questions. "How come you like Noreen so much?"

Without answering, Rodney returned to staring out the window.

Oh, no, Calliope thought, he wasn't getting off the hook this time. She jabbed him with a sharp question. "Is it because Noreen reminds you of your mother?"

Rodney turned sharply to Calliope, glaring at her with watery red eyes. He probably didn't know it but he had answered at least one of her questions. She'd seen that look lots of other times. It was the look of a kid whose parents had just divorced.

"Stop talking about my mother," Rodney growled.

"I can talk about your mother if I want to," Calliope shot back.

"Oh no you can't—she's too good for you."

"Is that so?" snorted Calliope. "Maybe you hadn't noticed but we do live in the *same* neighborhood."

"Not my mother," Rodney crowed. "She lives in a big house now, just like Noreen."

So Calliope was right. Noreen did remind Rodney of his mother. Calliope studied Rodney, who had returned to looking out the window. He spoke again but this time as if making a promise to himself. "Someday I'm going to live in a grand house that has flowered wallpaper instead of grease on the walls."

"And that's why you like Noreen?" Calliope offered.

"Don't forget the Mercedes," Rodney added.

Oh, brother, thought Calliope with a sigh. How was she going to tell all this to Noreen?

Calliope 'Fesses Up

"Well?" Noreen sat cross-legged on her high bed, the captain perched on her shoulder. He cocked an eye down at Calliope, who squirmed at Noreen's feet.

Calliope knew that the captain and Noreen were awaiting an explanation. Why was it that Calliope and Rodney could both recite a poem about Noreen? But Calliope said not a word, just handed the torn and nibbled square of red construction paper to her friend.

Noreen took Calliope's offering between her index finger and thumb, holding the square out as if it were a snotty tissue. "What's this?" she asked suspiciously.

"It's the answer to your question," replied Calliope.

Noreen raised an eyebrow. "Must you always be so dramatic?"

Calliope shrugged. Asking her to forgo drama was like asking the sun not to shine.

With a sigh Noreen carefully unfolded the ragged scrap of paper and smoothed it out on the bed in front of her. The captain tilted his head until it aligned with the note's slanted type. After a moment he whistled like a sailor.

"Are you saying Rodney wrote this?" asked Noreen.

"He confessed on the ride home the other day." Then Calliope confessed herself, explaining how she'd plucked the note from Noreen's ice cream at the rink.

Calliope bowed her head, expecting a scolding. When none came she glanced up at her friend, who looked befuddled. "But why?" Noreen mumbled.

"I think," Calliope said, remembering the ride home with Rodney, "you remind him of his mom."

"Oh," murmured Noreen. She drew the note to her heart.

Head cocked like the captain's, Calliope eyed her friend. Noreen's left cheek wrinkled up as if trying to ride out the jab of a passing stomach cramp.

Calliope suspected she knew more about Rodney than she had let on. "What's the story with his mother, anyway?"

At first Noreen didn't answer. Then she whispered, "His mom ran off with another man."

"No kidding! Are you sure?"

Noreen nodded. "He was a friend of my dad's."

"Does this mother-stealer live in a mansion like yours?"

"Bigger."

Calliope's eyes grew wide as she tried to imagine a house bigger than Noreen's. She couldn't quite see the entire picture, but she was starting to get a clearer read on Rodney. Did he think that by living in a big house too he could win back his mother? Maybe that was why he was saving up all that change.

" 'Somewhere, over the rainbow,' " Captain Tweakerbeak crooned, " 'bluebirds fly.' "

Calliope smiled sadly at the captain. "He's right, you know."

"What do you mean?"

"Rodney is like Dorothy, dreaming of a better life in a faraway land."

"Hmm," said Noreen.

Had Noreen heard Calliope? She doubted it, given the faraway look in Noreen's eyes. Calliope poked her foot. "Earth to Noreen, over."

Noreen turned slowly to face Calliope, a corner of her mouth twisted up in a wicked half smile. "Do you want to do something really naughty?"

Oh, no. Calliope preferred to sit upright in a hard wooden chair and smile sweetly.

Beauty Hurts

With the captain as her helmsman, Noreen led Calliope on a winding journey through the bowels of her house, eluding both Louisa and Mrs. Catherwood. They ended up in front of a door on the opposite end of the long hallway from Noreen's room.

Calliope followed her friend into a room that was most unlike Noreen's. It had pink walls adorned with the gleaming white-toothed faces of television, movie and pop-music stars. But what really caught Calliope's eye was a vanity. It had a big mirror that reflected a desktop cluttered with crusty-lipped makeup bottles. "Whose room is this?" Calliope asked in amazement.

"Ashley's."

Of course! Noreen's college-age sister, remembered Calliope. Ashley was a girl who let boys write poems about her underwear.

Noreen kneeled in front of the vanity and the captain hopped off her shoulder. He strutted in front of the mirror, cackling, "Pretty boy, pretty boy."

Noreen rifled through a deep drawer. "I know it's here somewhere. Aha!" she exclaimed, withdrawing a silky pink box studded with little plastic hearts from the drawer. Still kneeling, she caressed the box. Gingerly she lifted the wobbly lid. Inside was a stack of letters, cards and scraps of paper not unlike the red note. She withdrew a card in the shape of a flashy automobile.

"What's that?" said Calliope.

"Guess."

"A love poem to Ashley?"

Noreen nodded. "Do you want to hear what it says?"

"Should we?"

"Just this one."

"All right," said Calliope, plopping down cross-legged next to Noreen.

"You are the waxy shine on my car," read Noreen. "The silvery gleam of its hubcaps after I wash them."

"Not bad," said Calliope, stroking her chin. "Still . . ."

"Not half as good as Rodney?" offered Noreen.

Exactly, thought Calliope. She wondered if Noreen was thinking what she was, that there was something irresistible about a boy who longed for his mother and wrote poetry—even if he was mean to Calliope. Could such a boy ever like a girl who played with Barbie heads and talking parrots? Calliope said nothing of this to Noreen but instead asked, "Why do you think boys like Ashley so much?"

Noreen pointed her sharp nose up at the ceiling, lost in thought. "Perhaps," she said finally, "it was her smell."

"Her smell?"

"Yes," said Noreen, definitively this time. Her nose sniffed and then she motioned for Calliope to do the same.

Calliope closed her eyes, tilted back her head and breathed deeply. Her nostrils twitched with a faint smell that was a mixture of baby powder and lilacs. "Hmm," murmured Calliope, smiling. She wouldn't mind hanging around Ashley one bit.

"Okay," said Calliope, opening her eyes, "what else?"

"Well," mused Noreen, "Ashley wore pretty flowered dresses, dusted her eyelids light blue and painted her lips red."

Picturing Ashley all dolled up gave Calliope a wonderful idea. "Let's dress up—"

"Like Ashley," added Noreen excitedly.

"And pretend we're going on a date!"

Why, You Little Devil

Noreen sashayed in front of the vanity mirror in a blue-flowered pink dress that hung down to her ankles. Batting her blue-painted eyelids at Calliope, she cooed, "Well?"

"Oh, Ashley," sighed Captain Tweakerbeak, sounding not unlike Scarlett in the movie *Gone with the Wind.*

"My turn," said Calliope, jumping up and edging Noreen away from the vanity. Calliope studied her creamy round face in the mirror. How did she want to make herself up? Not like a clone of Ashley, that was for sure.

Her fingers wandered through the junkyard of crusty makeup bottles. They finally stopped on a bottle of purple eye shadow. Perfect, she thought, opening the bottle and painting her eyelids.

"Oh, that's lovely," said Noreen in a tone suggesting she meant the opposite. She stood looking down her sharp nose at Calliope.

What did Noreen, who wore a white blouse and black skirt every day, know about makeup? Calliope ignored her friend and rouged both cheeks with red blush. Purple and red—now, that was a combo, thought Calliope, admiring herself in the mirror. Still, something was missing.

Again her fingers traipsed along the bottles, stopping this time at a jar of styling gel. She unscrewed the top and dabbed a finger in the goo. Yes, she thought, and scooped up a wad of gel on the tips of two fingers. Then she gathered up a handful of hair and slathered it with goo. In no time at all she'd fashioned the hair into a curved horn. She made a matching horn on the other side of her head.

"Why, you little devil," squawked the captain.

Calliope smiled, admiring herself in the mirror. She could also see the reflection of Noreen behind her, gazing in disbelief.

Now Calliope needed a matching outfit. She bounced into Ashley's deep closet. Minutes later she emerged, blue jeans draped across one arm, wearing a glittering purple leotard. "Look," she said, twirling in front of Noreen, "it fits perfectly."

"Ah, yes," Noreen said haughtily.

"And what's that supposed to mean?" Calliope said, stopping in midtwirl.

"Do you really think anyone would be caught dead with you looking like that?" Noreen pointed down at Calliope's leotard.

"What's wrong with the way I look?"

"Oh, nothing—except that you look like you're dressed up for Halloween as the dance instructor from Hades."

Calliope beamed at that.

"It wasn't a compliment," said Noreen.

"No? Well, at least I don't look like I'm wearing a flowered sack."

Calliope and Noreen glared at each other for a long moment. Then Noreen made a T with her hands. "Look, I know how we can settle this."

"Settle what?" said Calliope, playing dumb.

"Settle who gets to be Rodney's girlfriend."

"Who said anything about that?" said Calliope, sneering.

Noreen eyed Calliope with a faint smile and continued. "We'll bake cookies."

"Cookies?"

"Yes," explained Noreen. "We'll each bake Rodney a plate of cookies and whichever cookies he likes best will determine who gets to be his girlfriend."

This had to be a trick, thought Calliope. Noreen couldn't find the oven in her own kitchen, let alone bake. "No fair if Louisa helps."

"You think I can't make cookies?"

Calliope didn't answer.

"Well, I'll show you," sniffed Noreen. "Rodney's going to just love my cookies."

"Uh-huh," Calliope said skeptically. Calliope's marshmallow-chocolate-chunk cookies, made from scratch, were famous in her neighborhood.

"So is it a deal?" said Noreen, extending a hand.

Calliope spit into her palm and took Noreen's hand. "Deal."

Who's That Girl?

Calliope knew what Noreen was thinking. Go ahead, keep Ashley's purple leotard for the weekend if you want to. All the better to scare Rodney with.

But Noreen had it all wrong. Calliope was no devil. She was a glittering horned fairy. What lovesick poet wouldn't swap his typewriter for a chance to meet such an enchantress?

Noreen, of course, didn't understand poets. How could she, the poor thing? She was only slightly more imaginative than the white blouse she wore to school every day.

Calliope kept these thoughts to herself, instead indulging Noreen's fantasy of her as Devil Girl.

Devil Girl easily slipped her blue jeans over the glittering leotard. But there was no way to hide purple eye shadow and horns. She'd have to be snuck past Louisa and the Queen of Hearts, who would never approve of a girl leaving her castle looking like that.

Not to worry, Noreen assured her as she led Calliope through a warren of stairs and dark hallways. In no time they popped out a rear entrance. On the wall was an intercom and Noreen pushed a button. Charles appeared outside the door in the red Mercedes.

Calliope thought Noreen smiled a bit too sweetly as she waved good-bye to the Mercedes rumbling down the red-brick driveway.

No matter. She was free to test her costume on the outside world. Could she turn heads? She imagined glittering past a group of people, who all muttered among themselves, "Who's *that* girl?"

Sure enough, Calliope caught Charles peeking at her in the rearview mirror. She sat on the edge of her seat, turning her head so that Charles could get a good look at her. "Well, what do you think?"

"Having fun?" offered Charles.

True enough, but that wasn't what Calliope wanted to hear. She wanted Charles to gush and fawn and exalt her beauty.

Calliope slumped back into the seat, feeling a bit like Cinderella. The clock was ticking, she knew. Soon her eye shadow would start to smear and her horns to wilt. She was in a race against the fading magic of her costume.

In that race, going home would be a serious detour. Mom would greet her with a hurried hello as she rushed about with her Dustbuster. If Frederick was home he'd only try to crush her horns. And Jonah would study Calliope as if she were some witch doctor visiting from the Amazon jungle.

That was why Calliope didn't go inside when Charles dropped her off at home. She dallied on the front porch until the Mercedes disappeared around the corner. Then she dashed off toward Herschel's Deli, a couple of blocks away. Surely there'd be some boy inside buying a comic book or a bag of snacks on an early Saturday evening.

Inside she found a boy, all right. Only he had a grizzled face and wore a bloody apron. It was Herschel. He looked plenty scary but Calliope knew the truth. His trembling hand couldn't squeeze the juice out of a kosher pickle.

From behind his counter, Herschel eyed Calliope with a bushy eyebrow raised. Was he interested in her outfit? Calliope decided to find out. She raised her arms ballerina-style overhead and twirled. Her leotard glittered like a sparkler.

Herschel winced as if blinded. "Whatever happened to girls wearing pretty flowered dresses and pink bows?"

"Oh, Herschel, don't be so old-fashioned," chided Calliope.

Herschel shrugged. "I'm an old-fashioned kind of a guy. So sue me." With that, Herschel turned to cut open a box of snacks.

So much for coaxing Herschel into saying Calliope was pretty. She turned to scan the cramped deli for another potential admirer. Who she found instead was Kevin. He stood half-hidden among the racks of comics. In one hand dangled an opened bag of potato chips. The other held a rolled-up comic book. His greasy lips, flecked with bits of potato chips, formed a questioning O. He stared at Calliope as if she were some exotic beetle, exciting in its strangeness.

"What?" snapped Calliope. She couldn't stand Kevin's silent gawking another moment.

"Are you trying out for the Easter play at school?"

"No."

Kevin looked confused. "Then how come your eyes are purple and you're dressed funny?"

"Can't a girl dress up once in a while?"

"You mean," Kevin said, as if struggling with a new math concept, "for no other reason than to just do it?"

Well, when you put it like that, dressing up did sound dumb. Still, Calliope liked it. But she'd like it even more if someone other than herself thought she looked pretty. Her dad would have understood.

Make-believe Boyfriend

You'd have thought it was Easter Sunday. Noreen gleamed in her shiny black shoes and crisp white blouse. As for Calliope, she'd again donned her balloon pants and pink "Whatever" sweatshirt. Pretty festive, considering it was just a plain old Saturday.

The girls faced each other across the small table in Calliope's dinette. A heaping plate of cookies sat in front of each.

Calliope smirked at Noreen's cookies. Clearly Louisa had not helped her one bit. Dry and lumpy, Noreen's cookies could pass for wood chips.

As for Calliope's cookies, they were perfect disks, filled with hunks of gooey chocolate and marshmallows. She could barely resist eating one herself.

Noreen was beat before they'd even started, thought Calliope. But did she cry uncle? Anything but. She gazed at Calliope's plate as if it were empty.

From beyond the dinette Calliope heard a familiar *rizz,* which rose and fell, rose and fell. The sound signaled the approach of Calliope's mom. Sure enough, she appeared in the dinette's archway. In one hand she brandished a Dustbuster and in the other a palm-sized telephone.

"Mom, please," said Calliope, "can't you see we're busy?"

"Busy?" said Mom. She eyed the girls and the plates of cookies and frowned. "Tell me again why you baked the cookies?"

"We're expecting company, Mrs. Day," answered Noreen.

Calliope glared at Noreen but she knew it was hopeless. Noreen couldn't tell a half-truth if you wrote it out for her in large black letters and taped it to her forehead.

"Whoever it is must be pretty special," said Noreen's mom.

"Oh, he is," gushed Noreen.

"He?" said Mom. Her Dustbuster began to growl.

Calliope groaned to herself, eyes cast up at the ceiling. Why couldn't Noreen just say they were waiting for a friend, not a he?

"You mean," said Mom, waving the Dustbuster at the cookies, "all this is for a boy?"

"Not just any boy," Noreen politely corrected.

"No?" said Mom, looking anything but relieved by Noreen's assurance.

Noreen wagged her ponytail. "He writes poetry."

Mom's Dustbuster stopped growling and she smiled as if finally grasping the punch line of an inside joke. "That's sweet, but why today? Jonah's birthday isn't until next month."

"Eww," Noreen and Calliope whined in unison at the mention of Jonah's name.

"Who then?" said Mom, befuddled.

"Rodney," Noreen said dreamily.

"Rodney?" said Mom. "Auto garage Rodney?"

"Sure. I bet he's an artist just like his father." The voice belonged to Frederick, whose head suddenly appeared in the dinette's archway. "What Rodney's dad can do with a '67 Camaro is a work of art."

Frederick's nostrils twitched. He eyed Calliope's cookies with a wolfish grin.

Oh, great, thought Calliope, covering her cookies with both arms.

Eyes wide, Noreen stared up at Frederick as if he were indeed a giant wolf. She wasn't used to teenage brothers.

"Shoo," said Mom, revving her Dustbuster in Frederick's face. "Can't you see we're having girl talk?"

But Frederick didn't budge. His eyes locked on the cookies peeking out from under Calliope's protective embrace.

Calliope sighed. She knew there was only one way to get rid of Frederick. She picked one of the bigger cookies up off her plate and tossed it to her brother. There was a flash of teeth as Frederick snatched the cookie in midair. Cookie in mouth, he clomped out of the dinette. With relief Calliope heard him ascending to his attic lair.

Mom flashed Calliope a quick thank-you smile and then resumed grilling Noreen. "Now tell me, what do these cookies have to do with Rodney? It doesn't have anything to do with that red note from the other day, does it?"

Calliope and Noreen glanced furtively at each other.

"It's simple, Mrs. Day," Noreen assured her.

Calliope imagined Noreen as a cheery animated character who doesn't see the anvil dangling over her head. With bated breath she waited for Noreen to say something that would bring that anvil down on both of them.

"You see," Noreen explained, "Rodney will try both our cookies and pick the ones he likes best."

"And?" prompted Calliope's mom.

"If he likes my cookies, then I get to be his girlfriend. If he picks Calliope's, *she* gets to be his girlfriend."

"Girlfriend?" sputtered Calliope's mom. Her Dustbuster renewed its growling. "Aren't you girls a little young for dating?"

"Mom, please," erupted Calliope, cutting Noreen off before she could do any more damage. "It's just make-believe."

"It is?" said Noreen.

"Yea-ess," insisted Calliope, giving Noreen a hard look that silenced her. While still glaring at Noreen, Calliope addressed her mother. "It works like this, Mom. We send Rodney home and then go upstairs and dress up again—"

"Ah," cut in Mom, "just like last Saturday with the purple eye shadow."

"Exactly," said Calliope. "The winner pretends she's on a date with Rodney. The loser, of course, has to play Rodney."

"She does?" Noreen said, grimacing.

Thankfully Calliope's mom ignored Noreen for once. She eyed her daughter for a long moment and then asked, "Have you clued Rodney in on this game?"

"Eww, Mom, that's gross."

Calliope's mom revved her Dustbuster, which sounded as if it were muttering "Yes . . . no, yes . . . no."

She bit her lower lip as if struggling to accept the truth of her daughter's explanation. "Sometimes I swear you're nine going on forty," she said. With a wave of her Dustbuster, she turned to go. "All right. Rodney can come. But I'm going to be listening from the other room."

"Fine," said Calliope with a sigh. She watched her mother meander toward the living room, running her Dustbuster along anything within reach.

"Do you really think he'll come?" Noreen whispered across the table.

Calliope didn't answer, her eyes trailing her mother, who stopped in front of the couch that sat between the two front windows.

Gazing out the window, Mom vacuumed the sill again and again.

"Yeah," Calliope finally answered Noreen, "if my mom doesn't scare him away."

Noreen turned to watch Calliope's mom too. "Calliope?"

"Huh?"

"Were you serious?" asked Noreen, turning back to eye Calliope.

"About what?"

"About just pretending the winner is going out on a date with Rodney?"

Calliope faced Noreen, smiling wickedly. "What do you think?"

No Contest

Sure enough, Rodney showed up, although he took his sweet time in arriving, if you asked Calliope. She'd given up all pretense of patience and had taken to pacing back and forth behind her seat at the dinette table.

In contrast, Noreen sat calmly, hands folded on the table in front of her, and gazed out the dinette's windows at Calliope's mom's thicket of a garden.

At the sound of the doorbell, Calliope rushed to the dinette's archway and peered out toward the front door. She couldn't quite see the door around her mother. But she heard her mom greet Rodney.

"I hear you're quite the poet."

"What?" replied Rodney.

Rodney's modesty surprised Calliope. Was it to impress her mother? That sounded like something he might do.

"Oh . . . right," said Rodney, recovering, after an awkward silence. "Thank you, Mrs. Day."

Calliope raced back to her seat as she heard her mom lead Rodney into the dinette.

When he entered, the first thing Calliope noticed was his bow tie. She'd never seen it so ungreasy. And it was almost straight. Did Rodney suspect something other than a cookie tasting?

In one hand Rodney held an invitation. Calliope had given it to him in school, explaining it was her way of making up for stealing his poem. And yes, she'd done as he'd asked, giving Noreen the poem and saying what a swell guy he was.

Rodney had accepted the invitation, beaming.

Calliope had made it herself, fashioning a replica of a giant chocolate chip cookie out of brown construction paper. Inside the paper cookie Noreen had written in precise small letters that they needed him to help choose what recipe to enter into a contest at the YWCA.

Rodney laid the invitation down on the table and hungrily eyed the plates of cookies. "Where do I begin?"

"Just a moment," said Calliope. She looked up at her mother, who stood behind Rodney, and wriggled her fingers in a gesture of good-bye.

"All right, I'm going," said her mom, "but I'll be within earshot."

The moment her mother disappeared into the living room, Calliope pushed her plate of cookies at Rodney. "Why don't you start with these?"

Rodney glanced at Noreen, who gracefully nodded her consent. He picked up one of Calliope's cookies as if against his better judgment. He turned the cookie over and over. What did he expect to find? Dead flies instead of chocolate chips? He raised the cookie to his nose and sniffed.

"That's it," erupted Calliope. "Just taste it, will ya?"

Again Rodney glanced at Noreen, who nodded. He nibbled a corner of the cookie. His eyes twinkled and the cookie disappeared into his mouth like a branch into a wood chipper. He grabbed another cookie and then another and another. Soon crumbs encrusted his lips and Calliope's plate was half empty.

Calliope smiled triumphantly.

"Oh, Rodney," Noreen purred. "Aren't you forgetting something?"

"Sorry," said Rodney, and grabbed a lump off Noreen's plate. Without inspection he tossed it into his mouth.

At first Rodney tried to smile as he chewed. But it took every muscle in his mouth to grind up Noreen's lump masquerading as a cookie. Around and around and around went his jaw. Finally he gave up trying to grind the cookie into submission and just swallowed. His eyes bulged as the cookie went down.

"Well?" said Noreen.

"Is there any milk?" Rodney croaked, his face reddening.

"Sure," said Calliope, popping up out of her seat. She returned moments later with a big glass of milk.

Rodney snatched it out of her hand, slopping milk

onto his sleeve. He drained the glass, head thrown back, gulping like a tree toad.

"Well?" Noreen asked again, this time more insistently.

Rodney put down his empty glass. Without hesitation he declared, "I pick Noreen's cookies."

"What?" blurted out Calliope.

"Now, Rodney," Noreen said, glancing at Calliope, "are you absolutely sure?"

"Oh, yeah," said Rodney, "no contest."

"No contest?" Calliope jumped up out of her seat. "You nearly choked to death."

"Now, now," tutted Rodney, "don't be a sore loser."

"Sore loser my—"

"Calliope," Noreen cut in with a harsh whisper, nodding toward the living room, where Calliope's mom was surely eavesdropping.

Calliope bit her tongue until it hurt. Calming, she grumbled, "Let me see one of those cookies," and then swiped one off Noreen's plate. She popped the cookie into her mouth as Noreen looked on, smiling.

Geez, thought Calliope as she chewed. Noreen's cookies could choke a beaver. What had she used for batter, Silly Putty?

Her tired jaws slowed and she had a depressing thought: Rodney must really like Noreen. Why else would he say her cookies tasted good? In defeat Calliope spit the mauled cookie out onto her plate. "All right, you win."

"You mean it?" said Noreen, apparently not expecting Calliope to cave without a scene.

Calliope plopped back into her seat, letting her head droop onto an upraised palm.

Smiling faintly, Noreen looked up again into Rodney's face. "Rodney," she cooed.

"Uh-huh?" Rodney said dreamily.

"Would you recite another poem . . . about me?"

"You mean right now?" said Rodney.

Noreen signaled yes through a slight widening of her smile.

"Uh . . . I don't have any more. I'll have to make up a new one."

"Well, go ahead."

"I can't do it right here. I need . . . a typewriter." Rodney pronounced the word triumphantly.

The corners of Noreen's lips turned down in the slightest of pouts.

"No problem," said Calliope, standing.

"Huh?" said Rodney.

Calliope didn't explain but dashed upstairs. She returned moments later with Jonah's little typewriter, clanging it down on the table in front of Rodney.

Calliope sat back down and she and Noreen looked up at Rodney.

"I can't just write a poem here and now," he sputtered.

"Why not?" asked Noreen, raising her sharp nose.

"I'm an artist," huffed Rodney. "I have to wait for my muse to strike."

Consider it done, thought Calliope. She picked up

one of Noreen's cookies and bounced it off Rodney's head.

"Hey!"

"There," said Calliope, "the muse has struck. Now write."

The Poet's Lair

Would Calliope have won Rodney's heart if she'd baked silver dollars inside every one of her cookies? She considered the question as she sat alone atop the highest bar of a jungle gym in Pizza Park. Beneath her swarmed a playground of jubilant kids celebrating an unseasonably warm Saturday afternoon.

One girl in particular caught Calliope's eye. Feet braced against a bottom bar, she leaned out, letting the breeze flap her ponytail. A silvery clasp in her hair glittered like a fishing lure among the sea of kids.

Sure enough, Calliope saw a boy weaving his way toward the shiny clasp. He circled the jungle gym twice and then dove at the girl, giving her ponytail a good yank before speeding off across the playground.

The girl squealed but more in delight than in protest. Her smile welcomed the boy to try again. But, having had his fun, he rejoined his friends clustered around a seesaw.

And so it would have been with Rodney, Calliope decided. He would have gladly pocketed her silver dollars, only to choose Noreen's cookies just the same. Noreen could have served him chocolate-covered grasshoppers and he would have munched them down as if they were the finest peanut brittle. It wasn't Calliope's cookies Rodney disliked, it was the chef.

Well, ditto for her. Rodney was smart, all right. But Calliope didn't care for the way he used his smarts. He tricked people. People like her.

Rodney, Rodney, Rodney. Surely he wasn't the only boy who wrote poetry, Calliope told herself. Lots of kids had divorced parents. Had it brought out the poet in other boys?

Calliope looked hopefully across the playground. She saw boys battling each other with stick swords. Others wrestled in the dusty grass. And still others ran alone in circles. Not a one struck her as poet material.

She cast her eye farther afield. Her gaze came to rest on a lone turtle the size of a picnic bench at the back of the playground. This turtle, a weave of metal bars topped with a flattened shell as a seat, had been Calliope's first jungle gym. Apart from the main playground, it sat rusting and forgotten. So why, then, could she make out a hunched figure through the side bars of the turtle? She craned her neck for a closer look and noticed that the figure wore a tweed jacket.

Rodney, playing in the dirt? Not likely, given that his room didn't have a speck of dust. He must be hiding, concluded Calliope. But from what? That was for Rodney to know and Calliope to find out.

She monkeyed down off the jungle gym and circled toward Rodney. Hidden behind a screen of bushes, she imagined herself a tiger creeping up on an antelope grazing with its head down. Indeed Rodney didn't look up once as she neared.

At a thick tree trunk Calliope stopped. She studied Rodney's back. Could she get atop the turtle without him noticing her? It couldn't hurt to try.

She slunk up and on top of the turtle. Slowly she flattened herself belly first against the rusting metal and pressed an eye against a slit in the shell.

Rodney was sitting cross-legged, chewing on the eraser of a yellow pencil. A notepad rested on his right knee.

So it was true, thought Calliope, rolling over onto her back and looking up at the wide blue sky. Rodney was indeed the author of that wonderful poem. She'd had her doubts when he couldn't write anything on Jonah's typewriter last Saturday. Now she'd caught him, evidence in hand, in his poet's lair.

Who would have thought? Calliope chuckled. Mr. Clean found his muse in the dirt under a rusting metal turtle in Pizza Park. Wait till she told Noreen. But first things first. She wanted to watch an artist at work. She rolled over, again pressing her eye on the slit.

Rodney's notepad was blank. Pelting him with a cookie hadn't reawakened the sleeping muse inside his head. She must have flown south for the winter, Calliope thought, and giggled to herself.

Rodney sighed and raised his head a half inch, revealing a dog-eared notebook teetering on his left knee. "Come on, come on," he grumbled, flipping through the pages. Suddenly he stopped, smiling at the page between his fingers. Then he began writing on the pad on his right knee, keeping one eye on the page in the notebook.

There was no mistaking that dog-eared notebook. Calliope had seen Kevin scribbling in it a thousand times in class. Again she pictured him trying to shield it from Rodney's prying eyes. Had Rodney finally persuaded Kevin to lend him his notebook? It seemed unlikely, given how Kevin clutched it to his side at all times. But why, then, would Rodney steal Kevin's notebook? There wasn't any big test coming up and surely Rodney wouldn't find Kevin's endless class notes interesting.

The mystery vexed Calliope but she didn't intend to stay vexed for long.

The Stolen Notebook

Calliope dropped her head over the side of the turtle and boomed, "Hello!"

Her move surprised Rodney as planned. He bounced up, banging his head on the top of the turtle. The notebook slid off his knee and Calliope reached out to grab it. Notebook in hand, she jumped to her feet.

"Hey!" cried Rodney, scrambling out from under the turtle. He lunged at Calliope but she dodged his hands.

Winded, Rodney retreated a step and then growled, "Give me back my notebook."

"*Your* notebook?" challenged Calliope.

"Yeah," said Rodney without conviction.

She raised an eyebrow.

"Well . . . Kevin lent it to me."

"Oh, really?" scoffed Calliope.

"Yes, really."

"Why?"

"I don't have to tell you," said Rodney.

"Fine," said Calliope, turning to jump off the turtle. "I'll just ask Kevin myself."

"No—wait."

"Yes?" said Calliope, turning back to face Rodney.

"You know how I stink at social studies. Well, Kevin was kind enough to lend me his notes to study for Monday's test."

"Yes, you do stink at social studies but there isn't any test Monday."

Calliope watched the muscles of Rodney's jaws move as if he was grinding his teeth. She wagged the notebook at him. "If you want this back, you'd better tell me the truth."

Rodney raised his arms as if preparing to lunge at Calliope again but he didn't. Instead he flicked a hand at her. "All right, I'll tell you the truth—but you're not going to like it."

"Oh? And why's that?"

"Because I think Kevin has been stealing my poems."

The notebook nearly slipped out of Calliope's grasp.

"At first I didn't believe it myself," said Rodney.

"You're full of it," said Calliope, regaining her grip on the notebook.

Rodney nodded at the notebook. "Go ahead, see for yourself."

"I'll do just that," said Calliope, opening the notebook while keeping an eye on Rodney. But she forgot all about him as she flipped through the pages.

What she found inside the notebook stunned her. There were no math problems or notes on the American colonists. Instead Kevin's notebook was filled with page after page of doodling, passages copied from books and snippets of funny conversations overheard in class.

Calliope stopped at a drawing that filled a page. It was of Mrs. Perkins, her stick-thin arms and legs flailing, falling backward as she missed her stool. Geez, thought Calliope, maybe Kevin wasn't such a goody two-shoes after all.

"Keep going," nudged Rodney.

Calliope didn't need any encouragement. Her fingers raced through the pages while she wondered what would turn up next. Then she stopped again, this time to study a full-page poem. "Your knees are wobbly," Calliope read softly, and the notebook sank in her hands.

"I told you," crowed Rodney. He extended a hand to Calliope, his fingers beckoning for the return of Kevin's notebook.

But Calliope didn't surrender it. She couldn't bring herself to concede that Rodney was right. Yet Calliope had to admit it didn't look good for Kevin. He'd copied down all this other stuff. Why not Rodney's poem? There was only one way to find out for sure.

She jumped down off the turtle.

"Hey!" protested Rodney.

But Calliope didn't heed his call to stop. She ran toward Kevin's house on the other side of Pizza Park.

Spy Family Romanoff

Kevin's house looked like a slumbering brontosaurus. Its long wooden frame sprawled across an entire corner of the block.

Notebook clutched to her chest, Calliope huffed up the tall steps to a simple glass door. She peered through the glass and rang the doorbell. She half-expected a maid to answer, as at Noreen's.

It wasn't a maid who answered. A scraggly old cat meandered to the door, sat back on its haunches and stared up silently at Calliope.

The kitty looked friendly enough, so Calliope opened the unlocked door and stepped inside. "Here, kitty, kitty," said Calliope, stooping to pick up the cat. But it jumped through her free arm and headed farther into the house.

Calliope followed. She began to feel a bit like Alice following the White Rabbit down the hole. The scraggly old cat led her through a maze of narrow passages and small rooms. There weren't any talking doorknobs but Kevin had other stuff equally strange. Red, white and orange cables sprouted from holes in the wall and ran stapled along the baseboards. She passed a room filled with computers blinking red, white and yellow numbers. Over the computers hung a bank of small televisions mounted on the wall, each tuned to a different channel.

This wasn't the White Rabbit's burrow but James Bond's hideout. What if Kevin and his family were a nest of spies—like in that movie, *Spy Family Romanoff*? That would explain all Kevin's note taking.

Boy, wouldn't it be exciting if Calliope was right?

Heart pounding, Calliope followed the kitty into one room and out of another. Finally they reached a wide archway that opened onto what looked like a living room. There, sitting on a long puffy couch, was Kevin, wedged between a man and a woman. Had he been captured by enemy agents?

Calliope silently hung back in the archway, listening. The kitty sat at her feet, listening too.

The woman held last week's math test in her hand. A red A– glowed atop the paper. "I'm a little disappointed," she said. Her tone was more sad than harsh.

Kevin listened, chin buried in his chest, studying his frayed sneakers.

"We know you can do better," said the man, draping an arm across Kevin's shoulders.

Do better? It had been a very hard test, remembered Calliope. Her mom had been jubilant about Calliope's B+.

Kevin was trapped, all right, but not by enemy

agents. These were his parents. Calliope decided to come to Kevin's rescue—if only accidentally, so to speak.

The kitty must have been thinking the same thing, for it suddenly meowed.

All heads on the couch turned to face the kitty and then Calliope.

"My notebook!" Kevin jumped up and rushed over to her. She handed him the notebook and he received it as if she had returned a long-lost favorite stuffed animal. "Where'd you find it?"

"In the park."

"Pizza Park?" Kevin sounded mystified. He caressed the frayed edges of his notebook, lost in thought.

"Kevin?" It was Mrs. Jefferson.

"Hmm?" Kevin replied absentmindedly.

"Won't you introduce us to your friend?"

"It's Calliope," said Calliope, stepping out from behind Kevin. "Calliope Day."

"Calliope?" said Mrs. Jefferson, "as in the Greek Muse?"

"Exactly!" It wasn't every day Calliope met someone who understood the meaning of her name. She remembered the bundled cables, televisions and Kevin's notebook. Had he been spying on her, reporting back to his spy parents? "How'd you know that?" she asked suspiciously.

Mr. Jefferson beamed. "Kevin's mother did her Ph.D. work in Greek mythology at Harvard."

"You mean Harvard as in University?" said Calliope.

With a laugh, Mrs. Jefferson said, "Now it's my turn to be impressed. How would you know about Harvard at your age?"

"My brother Jonah wanted to go there," said Calliope, "but Mom said we couldn't afford it."

"I'm sorry to hear that," said Mrs. Jefferson, sounding truly sorry. She addressed Kevin. "Why don't you invite Calliope to lunch? That's the least we can do to thank her for finding your notebook."

"Can I?" Kevin exploded, and then, seeing his parents' look of surprise, turned to stare down at his sneakers.

You bet Calliope wanted to stay for lunch. How else would she learn whether Kevin had written the poem to Noreen and whether his family were really Russian spies? Raising her nose ever so slightly, she said in her best imitation of Noreen, "You're too kind. If it's not an inconvenience, I'd love to stay for lunch."

Kevin looked up from his sneakers, head cocked back to study Calliope. She imagined him puffing out "Who . . . are . . . you?" like the big caterpillar in *Alice's Adventures in Wonderland.*

Calliope could have asked the same of him.

Death by Butter Knife

"Well," said Mr. Jefferson, rising with a slap of his khaki-clad thigh. "I'd better be getting back to work."

On a Saturday? Very suspicious, thought Calliope, her eyes tailing Mr. Jefferson as he disappeared through the dark maze of hallways.

Calliope turned back to see Kevin anxiously eyeing his mother.

Mrs. Jefferson rose but she didn't leave. "I know," she said brightly, "I'll make you tuna salad with carrots, celery and sprouts on nine-grain bread."

Mmm, sprouts. Calliope had tried those once. They had a taste that reminded her of the time she'd fallen face first out of a tree and gotten a mouthful of grass.

Luckily Kevin wasn't partial to sprouts, either. "Mom, if you don't mind, I think we'll just make ourselves a couple of PB and J sandwiches."

Calliope endorsed Kevin's proposal by nodding enthusiastically.

Although she looked disappointed, Mrs. Jefferson didn't persist. But neither did she go away. She followed them down another dark passage. The passage emptied into a cavernous room with a brick floor.

They could have been standing in the kitchen at Grunting's, a restaurant where Calliope and her mom often stopped for lunch while running errands. Like Grunting's, this room had a great steel grill with a dozen burners. Long, unpainted wooden planks formed the counter. Looming against one wall stood a tall icebox with sliding glass doors. The other walls were paneled with cabinets.

Calliope must have been gawking, for Kevin proudly explained his restaurant of a kitchen. "My dad bought all this stuff from a place that was going out of business."

"So your dad is a chef?" Calliope sounded a bit disappointed.

Kevin and his mother smiled in unison.

"What's so funny?" grumped Calliope, wondering if she'd somehow said something stupid.

"My dad could burn water," explained Kevin. "He just thought it would be fun to have a kitchen that looks like a restaurant."

Kevin's restaurant kitchen turned out to be not as fun as it looked. Its vast cabinets held not a single chip or cookie. The peanut butter Mrs. Jefferson set out was as thick as school paste.

There was plenty of bread but it was either brown or lumpy with nuts. Finally Kevin found four slices of white bread crystallized with freezer burn. They were buried at the bottom of the fridge as if banished to Siberia. "I've been saving these for a special occasion," he confided.

Mrs. Jefferson dogged her son's every step as he assembled bread, peanut butter and jelly. Her eyes bulged as she watched Kevin stab a dull knife into the jar of peanut butter. The knife stuck like the Sword in the Stone and Kevin struggled to pull it out. Mrs. Jefferson leaned forward, hands outstretched. She looked ready to throw herself in front of the knife should Kevin slip and plunge the dull blade toward his heart.

Not even Kevin could be that big a klutz. Calliope recalled the last time she'd made herself a PB and J sandwich. She chuckled at the memory of herself twirling the butter knife on the tip of her index finger. Mrs. Jefferson would never let Kevin do something like that, and Calliope's heart sank a little bit for him.

"Mom," Kevin asked, having survived the sandwich making, "would it be all right if we ate in my room?"

"Well . . ." Mrs. Jefferson hesitated.

"I promise we'll leave the door open so you can check on us if you want," Kevin added quickly.

"All right, then."

That's it, thought Calliope, no warning against smearing jelly on the carpet or bedsheets? That was what Calliope's mother would have pestered them about. She wouldn't have cared less whether the door of Calliope's room was open or shut.

Following Kevin out of the kitchen, Calliope glanced back at Mrs. Jefferson. By the sad look on her face you'd have thought Kevin was leaving her and going away on an African safari. And, in a way, it turned out they were.

The Electronic Graveyard

Ha! And her mother thought Calliope's room was messy. Compared to Kevin she was the Queen of Clean. Kevin's room looked like the elephants' dying ground in old Tarzan movies. But instead of elephant bones, the skeletal remains of televisions, computers and VCRs lay strewn across the floor. Scattered among the hunks of electronic parts were books, comics and papers.

Calliope surveyed this graveyard from the doorway. Kevin stood next to her, using his notebook as a tray for their sandwiches. "I like to see how things work," he said, shrugging at his messy floor.

"I guess." Calliope's eyes searched for a clear spot to sit and eat. Her gaze stopped on the oddest picture she'd ever seen. Well, not a picture, actually, although it was framed and hung from the wall. It was a glass-paneled box filled with neat rows of giant multicolored beetles, butterflies and who knows what else pinned to Styrofoam. In the top row was an orange beetle with giant pincers.

"Now I know what part of New Jersey your beetle

came from," said Calliope, pointing at the pinned orange monster.

Kevin gazed down sheepishly at his sneakers. "I was taking my African rhinoceros beetle to school for show-and-tell," he whispered.

"Sure you were," said Calliope, poking him in the ribs.

He smiled but didn't look up from his sneakers.

Calliope's stomach growled at her to find somewhere to sit and eat. The most promising place looked like a high bed set between two windows. Its smooth quilt rose like a high plain above the jungle floor.

Atop the bed sat the only whole computer in the room. It had a little blinking green light that beckoned Calliope to come sit. But Calliope doubted a rat skilled at running mazes could find a route through this mess.

Kevin must have heard Calliope's growling stomach. "Come on," he said, raising his notebook above his head as if preparing to ford a stream. He began high-stepping through the wrecked computers and TVs. Calliope pranced behind him.

Three feet from the bed Kevin stopped, steadied himself and then lunged toward it. He landed on top, spilling the sandwiches onto the quilt. Calliope leaped after him, belly flopping onto one of the sandwiches.

"I'll eat that one," offered Kevin, picking up the squashed sandwich. He set both sandwiches on his notebook and then laid the notebook on top of the computer, setting it between them. "Lunch is served."

Such a gentleman, thought Calliope, although she didn't say so.

They sat cross-legged across from each other and bit into their sandwiches. Thank goodness for the jelly. Otherwise Calliope doubted she would have been able to swallow a bite. The sandwich reminded her of Noreen's cookies.

"Sorry," mumbled Kevin. "I guess we should have stuck with the tuna salad." He gobbled down his sandwich so fast that his tongue probably didn't have time to taste it.

It looked like a good strategy to Calliope and she followed suit. After all, it wasn't Kevin's cooking that interested her but his family. She had a million questions to ask him. "How come your parents have all those wires, computers and televisions?"

"That's their office."

"You mean they work out of the house?"

"Uh-huh."

"So no one will see them?"

"Well, I don't know about that."

"I do," said Calliope, winking at Kevin.

Kevin's eyebrows knitted but his confusion looked a little too contrived to Calliope.

"I knew it," she pronounced. "You *are* the spy family Romanoff."

"We're the what?"

Calliope leaned forward, whispering conspiratorially. "What side are you on—ours or the Russians'?"

For a moment Kevin stared in disbelief. Then he began to giggle.

"What?" said Calliope, sitting up straight.

"My parents aren't spies."

"No?"

"They're money managers."

"Is that like spying?" asked Calliope hopefully.

"I wish," said Kevin.

"Then what is it?" said Calliope. Although disappointed, she was still intrigued.

"It's when you buy and sell stocks and bonds for other people."

Hmmm, thought Calliope, stocks and bonds. Still sounded pretty mysterious—and that was good enough for her. She pronounced Kevin and his family most intriguing, her highest compliment.

But Kevin didn't say thank you. He didn't even appear to be listening to Calliope anymore. He stroked his notebook and murmured, "I must have dropped it in the schoolyard on the way home."

"I don't think so," said Calliope.

Kevin looked up at her. "What do you mean?"

Confession Time

"Stolen?" Kevin's brow wrinkled as if resisting the idea. But in a moment he gave in, his forehead uncreasing. "Rodney?"

Calliope nodded.

"Man," said Kevin, pounding his notebook. "I don't get him. Why is he so interested in my stuff?"

"It's not to cheat on any test," quipped Calliope. She immediately regretted her wisecrack.

Kevin's chin sank like a lead sinker to his chest. Twisting a lock of hair, he stared down at the notebook. "You didn't read it, did you?"

Calliope's face flushed with embarrassment. "Well, I couldn't help it," she whined in defense.

"Oh no?" Kevin grabbed the upper corners of his notebook, sealing it tight against the computer.

"Kevin?"

He didn't answer but stared down at the notebook as if it were the only thing in the room.

"I have to ask you a really important question," pressed Calliope.

"What?" Kevin said grumpily without looking up.

"Did you write a poem about Noreen?"

"No."

"Are you absolutely sure?"

"Of course I'm sure," rasped Kevin.

"Oh, man," sighed Calliope, "so it *is* true."

"What's true?"

"You stole that poem from Rodney."

"What!" Kevin looked up sharply from his notebook.

"Stop," protested Calliope, embarrassed by Kevin's feeble pretense of ignorance.

"I have no idea what you're talking about," insisted Kevin.

"Oh yeah?" Calliope swept Kevin's hands from the notebook and threw it open. She flipped to the page with the poem about Noreen. "Okay, then what's this?"

Kevin's eyes bulged at the sight of the poem.

"You *did* copy this poem from Rodney."

"I did not!"

"Kevin, please," said Calliope, rising to go in disgust.

"*I* wrote this poem and it isn't about Noreen," bellowed Kevin, thrusting a pointed finger down at the open notebook.

Calliope had rarely heard the soft-spoken Kevin speak so loudly. His words now hit her like a gust of hot air, knocking her back on her haunches. Her eyes obeyed his pointing finger and looked at the page opened between them. This time she read the whole poem, right down to the last line, which read: "When you're Calliope, my Calliope, you skate as you please.

Calliope, my Calliope, would you please skate with me?"

Calliope swallowed hard. So she'd had it all backward. It was Rodney who'd copied the poem from Kevin, inserting Noreen's name for her own. That was why he couldn't write a poem at Calliope's house the other day. He wasn't awaiting inspiration. Just an opportunity to swipe another poem from Kevin.

She glanced sheepishly up at Kevin. If he never spoke to her again she wouldn't blame him.

But Kevin looked anything but angry. He'd lost steam like a cooling radiator and had returned to staring at the notebook. Meekly he asked, "You're not mad, are you?"

"Me, mad? About what?"

"You know . . . me writing a poem about you."

Calliope waved off the question as if Kevin were crazy. But what did she feel? Embarrassed, that was for sure. But she also felt the relief that came with fitting the last piece of a challenging jigsaw puzzle.

And a new feeling crept up behind her, whispering in an ear: Kevin liked *her*—her!—not Noreen. The idea of it hit Calliope like a swinging door that catches you off guard, whacking you on the back of the head.

Finally! A boy had noticed her. But now what? Did she feed Kevin carpet fuzz and Cheerios and put him back in his cage if he got out of hand? That was what she did with Mortimer, the only other boy she knew who liked her. Somehow Calliope didn't think carpet fuzz would satisfy Kevin.

Heck, she didn't even know if she liked Kevin. He certainly wasn't anything like her father. Dad could charm the broom away from the Wicked Witch of the West. Kevin, on the other hand, could barely get up the nerve to say hello to Calliope, let alone say he liked her. Yet he'd written this wonderful poem.

Kevin really was the *mystery* poet.

"Nobody gets you, do they?" said Calliope, speaking for herself as well.

Kevin looked up from his notebook. "What do you mean?"

"I mean, all the kids think you suck up to the teacher, and Mrs. Perkins thinks you love to take down everything she says. But none of that's true, is it?"

Kevin shrugged, his eyes again drifting back down to the notebook. "I have a confession to make."

"Oh?" said Calliope.

"I did take something—but not from Rodney."

A Regular Pippi Longstocking

Kevin leaped off the bed, landing with a crunch among the electronic debris.

What now? wondered Calliope as she watched him root through his disemboweled computers, televisions and VCRs. Suddenly she heard a familiar sound among the clattering of metal and plastic. It was the jingling of small bells.

"My charm!"

Sure enough, there dangling from Kevin's fingertips were three bedraggled heads.

Kevin kneeled now, head bowed, as if awaiting a scolding.

But a scolding wasn't what Calliope had in mind. Her lost heads had helped her figure out what to do with this closet poet who fancied a girl who smelled faintly of rabbit and dill pickles.

"I know why you *borrowed* my charm," she teased.

Kevin glanced up.

"You wanted to write a poem about it, didn't you?"

"I did?"

She nodded, smiling down expectantly at him.

"You mean right now?"

Without answering, she curled into the bedspread like a cat getting ready to have its head scratched.

"All right," said Kevin, stroking the snarled braid of the charm as if it were a rabbit's foot. "I'll try." His gaze drifted up and for a long moment he studied the ceiling. Then he began to recite.

"No brothers Mario, nor Pikachu. No Sonic, no Zelda will do."

Kevin stopped, glancing over at Calliope curled atop his bed.

"Go on," she purred.

"When Calliope Day has something to say, Calliope Day says it her way."

Kevin's voice crescendoed, his eyes fixed on Calliope.

"She'll bind up three heads, add some bells, and then off she tingles, to raise a little . . . hell!"

"Kevin," Calliope pretended to scold, "such language!"

"Sorry," said Kevin, but he didn't look sorry at all. His gaze lingered on Calliope.

"What?"

"Well?" said Kevin.

"Well, what?"

"You know."

Calliope knew, all right. Kevin wanted to know if she liked his poem. No, scratch that. He wanted to know if she liked him.

Did she?

She certainly liked the picture he'd drawn of her with his words. Smart, free-spirited and brave. You'd have thought she was the Pippi Longstocking of Indian Trail Elementary.

Did that make Kevin her Mr. Nilsson, Pippi's faithful monkey companion who did everything with her? "How would you like to learn how to skate?"

Kevin frowned. "I know how to skate."

Calliope folded her arms in skepticism.

"I was that bad?"

Calliope nodded.

"Well, it was my first time."

"Do you think your mother would let you go again?"

"Maybe," said Kevin, smiling sheepishly up at Calliope, "if someone invited me."

Boy, poets didn't give up, did they?

Skate-Marching

Skating it was not. Maybe skate-marching. Kevin raised each skate high and then clunked it back on the scuffed wooden floor of Spackle's rink. Not once did Calliope see him actually roll.

She trailed behind him like a watchful mother following a toddler on a bike with training wheels. Will you please pay attention? Calliope muttered to herself as she watched Kevin. He clomped head down, writing in his notebook, paying little attention to the kids whizzing past him. He was an easy mark.

Sure enough, Bobby Applegate sailed out of nowhere and clipped Kevin on the shoulder. Kevin spun like a top, arms outstretched, his fingers clinging to his notebook. On the third spin he lost his balance and toppled down on his rear.

If the fall hurt either Kevin's bottom or his pride, he didn't show it. "Wow," he slurred, his eyes a bit crossed. "I've never done *that* before!" He slapped open his notebook on the floor and began writing again.

Calliope rolled up to him, the toes of her skates squeaking as they dug into the floor, trying to stop.

whatever

She stopped, all right—after slamming into Kevin and then toppling down beside him.

"Sorry," wheezed Kevin, winded more from writing than skating.

"It's not your fault. I still don't know how to stop," she scolded herself aloud. She rolled over to rest faceup on her raised elbows. Catching her breath, she studied the boy beside her. He was hunched face first into his notebook. "You don't get out much, do you?"

"Huh?" said Kevin without looking up.

"Never mind," said Calliope. Wearily she considered lifting him up for the fifth time and her arms quivered at the thought. "What do you say we get some ice cream?"

Kevin looked up with a pout. "No more skating?"

"Maybe later," said Calliope. She wobbled to a stand, then reached down and grabbed him by the elbow, guiding him to his feet. Together they clomped off the rink and collapsed onto the first carpeted bench outside the low wall.

"Hey, look," said Kevin, pointing to the cafeteria tables behind them.

Calliope turned to see Noreen sitting primly at a table. Beside her stood Rodney. He set a bowl of pistachio ice cream in front of Noreen and then tucked a napkin neatly under her chin.

Amazing, thought Calliope. Noreen hadn't raised her sharp nose in disapproval when Calliope had unmasked Rodney as thief rather than poet. But then again, Noreen had always liked her pancakes drenched in syrup and Rodney knew how to pour it on thick.

Noreen had turned him into a valet of sorts. She ordered him around as if training for the day she'd ascend to her mother's velvet throne. Rodney obeyed without complaint.

Watching Rodney fawn over Noreen made Calliope's skin crawl.

"Ice cream?" asked Kevin.

Well, maybe it wasn't fawning she objected to but the particular fawner. "Please," she said, smiling sweetly at Kevin.

Betty and Veronica

Noreen had a tree house that could turn Tarzan green with envy. It sat in a young oak in her backyard, equipped with TV, DVD player and popcorn popper. But what Calliope liked best was its big leather couch.

She draped herself now upside down on the couch, hair brushing the carpeted floor. In her hands she held a comic book Kevin had said she just had to read. It starred RoboBeetle, a mechanical bug that squashed a race of giant mutant houseflies.

Mutant houseflies, mechanical beetles? Kevin, Kevin, Kevin. A comic book connoisseur you are not. Calliope reminded herself to take Kevin to Herschel's and help him pick out a decent comic book. Say, something starring Wonder Woman. Now *she* was a superhero, outfoxing evildoers as much as giving them a good thrashing.

Calliope glanced up at Noreen. Her friend sat erect on the couch, face buried in a Betty and Veronica comic book. On the cover Archie, arms loaded with shopping bags, grunted as he trailed behind Veronica. In Calliope's eyes his face morphed into Rodney's. She almost felt sorry for the bow-tied Romeo.

"Noreen, are we through hating boys?" asked Calliope, sounding a bit disappointed.

"Don't be silly," said Noreen from behind her comic.

"Even Kevin and Rodney?"

Noreen lowered her comic, revealing a sly smile. "Kevin and Rodney are different."

"How so?" Calliope sounded skeptical.

"They're not boys."

Not boys? Now, that would be news to Rodney and Kevin, Calliope suspected. "Noreen, what are you talking about?"

"Look," said Noreen, sounding gently superior like Mrs. Perkins. "Boys are scabby, smelly things, right?"

"Duh."

"And they live to torment girls."

No argument there. "So what's your point, Noreen?"

"Well, does Kevin torment you?"

"No."

"Does he smell?"

"Not particularly."

"See?" said Noreen, smiling at Calliope. "He's not a boy."

Calliope swung herself right side up on the couch. "Okay, Miss Smarty-pants," she challenged. "If Kevin is not a boy, then what is he?"

"A friend."

Noreen had a point. There were boys who didn't necessarily want to pull your hair or knock you down. There was Calliope's dad, for one. Was Kevin another? He certainly wasn't anything like her dad. But so what?

It was dawning on Calliope that boys, like girls, were as varied as seashells on a beach. For sure, some boys were like those shells that bristled with spikes. Step on one and you'd be sorry. Some girls were like that too. But other boys were like conches, harboring mysteries inside like the roar of the ocean. Those were the boys she wanted as friends.

No, from here on out, it was going to be hard, darn hard, to hate every boy who buzzed her at Spackle's. She might miss a friend well worth treasuring.

A friend, say, like Noreen. The two of them were like Betty and Veronica, as different as French vanilla and tutti-frutti ice cream, yet still the best of friends. Calliope's face twisted up in a funny smile as an idea popped into her head.

"What?" asked Noreen, noticing Calliope's smile.

"Let's make up our own comic book!"

"Really? About what?"

"Us, of course."

Noreen jumped up excitedly and ransacked the well-stocked tree house until she found a drawing pad and a purple crayon. "What should we call it?" She gnawed on the end of the crayon, lost in thought.

Calliope's eyes lit up. "How about . . . *Watch Out, World! Here Come Calliope and Noreen!*"

Noreen clapped her hands together. "I love it!" In bold purple letters, she wrote the title across the top of the page, extending the *e* of Calliope's name until it entwined the leg of the *N* in *Noreen.*

Whatever came next, they were in it together.

About the Author

Charles Haddad is a journalist for *Business Week*. This story, like *Meet Calliope Day* and *Captain Tweakerbeak's Revenge*, is set in his hometown, South Orange, New Jersey. Charles Haddad attended Sarah Lawrence College and Harvard University. He lives in Atlanta.